Missing in Egypt

**An Anna Davies Mystery
Book 1**

Rita Lee Chapman

**Missing in Egypt ©
Copyright R. Chapman 2011**

All rights reserved. No part of this publication may be reproduced or transmitted by any person or entity in any form or by any means, electronic or mechanical, including photocopying, recording, scanning or by any information storage and retrieval system without prior permission in writing from the publisher.

All characters in this publication are fictitious and any resemblance to any real person, living or dead, is purely coincidental.

Contents

Section 1 Life Decisions – Career Move

Missing	1
Kareem	15
Search for Ramy	25
The Ransom	34
Kareem's Disappearance	45
The Secret	55

Section 11 Life Decisions – Ramy's Story

Yasmeen	68
The Disagreement	84
The Secret Tomb	98
Golden Treasures	116

Section 111 Life Decisions – Mine

Valley of the Queens	121
What Lay Beyond	142
Back in Australia	156
Ramy's Story Continues	165
Fate's Next Twist	173
Hard Decisions	184

About the Author

Section I Life Decisions – Career Move

Missing

I was alone in the electorate office late one Friday afternoon when a well-dressed man of about thirty came in.

"Excuse me," he said "but I need Mr Blake's help."

I invited him to sit down and tell me how we could help.

"It's my brother," he explained "he's missing."

"I'm sorry to hear that," I replied "although missing persons are a Police matter so they really come under the State Government."

"No, you don't understand – my brother is missing in Egypt. We haven't been able to contact him for over a month and my family are crazy with worry about him."

"Oh, I'm sorry," I replied. "I didn't realise. Have you contacted the Australian Embassy in Cairo?"

"Yes, they say they are doing everything they can, but they cannot tell us anything."

As the story unfolded, it appeared that Kareem Hazif's younger brother, Ramy, had taken a few weeks holiday after finishing Uni to visit Egypt before he looked for a permanent job. He had been to Egypt once before, as a child, to visit his extended family there and was keen to return to see more of the country of his forebears. After staying with family in Cairo for a month he said he wanted to travel around by himself for a while and headed off up the Nile. Kareem said his family had received a postcard from Abu Simbel but there had been no contact since then.

"Ramy is usually very good at keeping in touch with regular postcards and phone calls, but no-one has heard anything since Abu Simbel," Kareem explained.

"Mr Blake is in Canberra at the moment, as the Parliament is sitting," I advised Mr Hazif. "However, I will be in contact with him and I know he will want to follow this matter up with the Minister for Foreign Affairs for you."

I tried to reassure him that young people can be very thoughtless when they are enjoying themselves but promised to contact him as soon as we received a reply from the Minister. I watched him leave the office. He was quite good looking, I noticed. Tall and well built he was wearing a dark suit and his white shirt highlighted huge brown eyes framed with long, dark eyelashes that most girls would die for. I typed up my case notes and prepared a letter to the Minister for Jim's signature. I placed it on the pile which Jim would sign over the week-end and called it a day.

As I sipped a hot chocolate at home curled up in my favourite chair, my mind slipped back to when I first went to work for Jim Blake and the learning curve that came with the job.

I'd been working in the City as Executive Assistant for the Group General Manager of a large corporation in Sydney – very prestigious, swish offices, an army of staff to assist with every request and a lovely boss. However, I hated the train travel and wasn't being stretched in my work. I was on the move! Then I saw the ad in the local paper – Personal Secretary to a Federal Member of Parliament – and close to home with parking!

At thirty years of age and single I, Anna Davies, had been ready for this new challenge. I owned my own home (well, at least a few bricks of it by now) and I was looking for a new career move. I was also looking for the chance to meet some new people (for "people" read "men"!)

The interview wasn't as terrifying as I had thought it would be. Tall and slim and wearing a very expensive looking suit he looked every inch the politician. I had done my research - Jim Blake was known as a hard-working Liberal Member with a reputation for working his staff as hard as himself and having an open-door policy to all his constituents. Father to two boys, aged fifteen and seventeen and a daughter of twenty-two he had little time for any hobbies and was a twenty-four hour a day politician. I was welcomed warmly by Lesley, his other staffer with whom I would be working and taken into Jim's office. Jim explained the requirements of the position, his expectations of me and asked me about my previous experience. He told me that his wife, Janine, had returned to work when the children were older and had a good career of her own as deputy principal of a local primary school. He was easy to talk to and I decided if I was offered the job I would take it.

It wasn't long after the interview that I heard the job was mine. On my first day I was both nervous and excited as I walked into the office of the local Federal MP. Right from the start I loved the job – it was very busy, very demanding and very interesting. I did find going from the private sector to a government job was very restrictive in some areas though. I was used to picking up the phone and ordering anything we needed but the government way of doing things – going through the department, completing paperwork and not always getting exactly what you wanted, could be very frustrating!

My work consisted of looking after the MP, making his appointments, keeping the diary, accepting or regretting invitations, arranging travel – flights, Commonwealth cars to and from the airport and to his appointments. I also looked after everything from stationery to coffee supplies. However, the major part of my job was helping constituents, particularly when Jim was out of the office or in Canberra when the Parliament was sitting. They would walk through the door - either premeditated or on a whim on their way past whilst out shopping - telephone or fax with a variety of problems from issues with Telstra, Social Security, Immigration, Veterans Affairs, Aboriginal Affairs – and everything else the Federal Government was responsible for running. Sometimes they just came in to give their views on a current affair or a position taken by the Opposition on an issue. In addition, I arranged telegrams for Silver, Golden and Diamond Wedding Anniversaries upon request from a family member. I also needed to be abreast of current political and government affairs in order to handle their inquiries. I soon began to wish I had a dollar for every time someone walked into the office and said "haven't you anything better to do?" as I struggled to scan the paper inbetween calls and mark off items of interest for Jim.

There were only two staff in the electorate office. My colleague, Lesley, handled the Liberal Party members and meetings, press releases and also some constituent work. Lesley was very outgoing, married to an architect and I suspected that she was keen to enter politics herself one day. At five foot four inches tall, with long dark hair and expressive brown eyes she was always very smartly dressed, her hair and make-up immaculate and she was always able to handle even the most difficult constituent with patience and flair – something I didn't always find easy!

After a few months it was suggested I go down to Canberra during a sitting week to see what happens in the Parliament House office. I certainly had plenty of butterflies on my first day at Old Parliament House! After putting my bag through the X-ray machine and passing through the scanner I was given a daily pass and some forms for Jim to sign for my permanent pass. The attendants were very helpful and directed me to Jim's office which turned out to be not much bigger than a broom cupboard. In the middle of the cupboard was a big desk, which we shared, sitting opposite each other. Fortunately Jim was out of the office most of the time, either in the Chamber or at Committee Meetings. He was very self-sufficient - and needed to be as he didn't have a member of staff in Canberra to assist him. The building was a rabbit-warren of little corridors and offices and it was easy to get lost. Jim gave me a tour, showing me the Chambers, Members' Private Rooms, the Party Room and the MPs' Dining Room. It was all very impressive.

I was in the office by nine and the House sat until six thirty, when it would break for dinner until eight o'clock and then sit until around eleven pm. Sometimes they would sit past midnight – occasionally there were even all-night sittings. There was a very good staff cafeteria which sold a large variety of food at very reasonable prices and here I met a few other staffers.

I was very conscious of having to think before I spoke of any political matters, especially if there were Labor party staffers around and even amongst our own colleagues. I was very lucky as usually Jim told me not to come back after six thirty, so I was free to return to my motel room, but I was still very tired at the end of each day. The staff of Ministers and Shadow Ministers were of course needed until the House rose. I learned on day one where the Press Boxes were as Jim was a prolific press release writer and I would climb up to the top level armed with about sixty copies of the press release and throw one into each box. Then we would wait to see if any of the papers picked up the story. It was a very exciting week for me and I loved every minute of it.

I had been with Jim for about a year when there was a Shadow Ministry reshuffle and Jim was appointed Shadow Minister for Immigration. This meant a much better office in Parliament House! The offices were allocated at the beginning of each Parliament and the longest serving MPs were given priority after the Shadow Ministers. We now had an office in the new annexe and it was very grand after the cupboard! We had a suite with two offices and three desks and a nice view over the Rose Garden! The other advantage was that we were now entitled to another staff member.

It was decided that, for the time being, we would put another person on in Sydney and I would go to Canberra for the sitting weeks.

It was much more pleasant working in our new environment. As a Shadow Minister Jim was very busy and now he really did need someone in Canberra when the House was sitting. The lady who took my photo for my new Pass commented "you all come in looking so fresh and within a couple of sittings you all look so worn out and tired."

Jim had always had a big interest in the immigration portfolio so we had a lot of inquiries and with his new title these increased fourfold as he dealt with cases Australia wide. As I found immigration very interesting I took on most of the Immigration caseload in the office.

Immigration seemed to bring out the best and worst in human nature and cultures. A Middle Eastern man came into the office one day.

"I want Mr Blake to help me speed up my relative's immigration application," he demanded.

"Certainly," I replied "when did you lodge it?"

The reply? "I'm lodging it tomorrow."

It was therefore a refreshing, if sad, experience when an Asian gentleman came in and, very apologetically, asked if we could find out what was happening with his young daughter's application.

"I'm so sorry to bother you, but she is living with my mother and she is very old," he said. "I know you are very busy and I very sorry."

"That's okay," I replied "we are here to help you. How long ago did you lodge the application?"

"Three years ago," was his response.

When I rang the Department it was ultimately decided that the application had somehow been lost and it was necessary for him to lodge a new one. We sent a letter in with the new application explaining the problems and it was very satisfying when his daughter finally arrived in Australia.

Every Department had a Parliamentary Liaison Officer who was the contact for MPs and their staff to help them through the departmental bureaucracy and provide quick and accurate responses to our inquiries. Ninety-five per cent of them were skilled professionals and without their help it would be impossible to service our constituents' inquiries. Of course there were always the odd exceptions who were not particularly helpful or quick, but the majority are a pleasure to deal with. (I'm sure they say the same about us!)

A lot of immigration inquiries were directed to Parliament House and a lot of my time was spent following up these cases. In addition, Jim often required me to research information for a speech – often at very short notice. It was nothing for him to say "I'm giving a speech in the House on so-and-so in an hour's time – see what you can dig up for me." The Parliamentary Library was wonderful for these occasions. They had a dedicated, hard-working staff who would happily pull out masses of information, which I could then sift through. There was of course a pecking order, which meant that the Ministers requests were given priority, then the Government MPs followed by the Opposition Ministers and lastly the Opposition backbenchers. It was just a matter of luck whether they were rushed off their feet at the time of your request. I discovered it certainly paid to be very nice to the researchers and to beg rather than demand in times of need! I was very proud when one of Jim's speeches, for which I had provided most of the material, was hailed by his colleagues as his best yet. (I think probably some credit should go to Jim's use of the material and his delivery!).

It was an odd life when Parliament was sitting. I would fly down Sunday night, stay in a motel all week, work odd hours and then fly back Friday morning the first week and Friday night the second week, when the House sat a day longer. The first week I would go straight from the airport to the Electorate Office and try to get on top of the Electorate work and then it would be back to Canberra again on Sunday night. Although we had a very good casual who came in for those weeks, I liked to do my own filing. If Jim needed something quickly I had to know exactly where to put my hands on it.

The highlight of the Parliamentary week was Wednesday evening, when the House rose at six thirty and everyone went out for dinner. I had become friendly with a couple of other girls and we usually went to one of the restaurants in Manuka Wednesday nights. Manuka was particularly popular and would be buzzing with groups of Parliamentary staffers and, quite often, Members as well. We were lucky that we also ate very well during the rest of the week as the staff canteen was exceptionally good, with many choices of hot and cold food, entrees, desserts, cakes for morning or afternoon tea, fruit and even small bottles of wine. Despite all the running around it was easy to put on weight.

By 1988 when the new Parliament House was opened I was no longer travelling down to Canberra for the Sitting weeks. Colleen was employed permanently in Canberra and she was very proficient in her role, with the added advantage of having previously worked in Parliament. In her thirties, Colleen was single and very popular around Parliament House. She was very tall, blonde and had piercing blue eyes that defied you to tell her an untruth. I know she was constantly being asked out by other staffers and politicians alike but she was smart enough not to mix politics with pleasure! It was Colleen who oversaw the move to the new building – the old Parliament House had become redundant. I must admit to feeling a little sad at the thought of never trotting down those famous halls again. She told me over the phone that when the guys came to move Jim he just waved his hands and said "put everything in exactly the same place in the new office" and left them to it.

The Parliament was formally opened by Her Majesty The Queen on 9 May 1988 and on the first sitting week in August there was to be an inaugural Dinner in the Great Hall, hosted by the Prime Minister, Bob Hawke. As Jim's wife was unable to attend due to another commitment in Sydney, Jim invited me along and I eagerly accepted. It was a good opportunity for me to familiarise myself with the new layout as I was still doing relief work in Canberra from time to time. What an amazing building! From its impressive entrance to its huge marble pillared forecourt, sweeping staircase up to the Members' offices and the beautiful Chambers it is an architectural marvel that all Australians can be proud to call their seat of Government. Much of it is made of glass and it is a very spacious, light and airy building. I marvelled at our *suite* of offices – a huge office for the Member, with ensuite; a large reception area and desk plus another office, a filing room and a kitchenette! In addition it is set in large grassed grounds overlooking the mountains. There are tennis courts for the use of Members and staff and underneath is a huge parking area.

By this time I was driving down to Canberra as I found it more convenient to have my car there and by the time I went to the airport and then waited for a car the other end, there was not much difference in the timing. It was tiring but it sure beat those occasions when a plane strike was called on a Friday evening, deliberately aimed at the politicians and we were all sitting at Canberra airport wondering if we were going to get home that week-end.

I went back to my motel and changed quickly and returned to the House. Drinks were served and as Jim was circulating I was left pretty much on my own. One of the other Shadow Ministers, whose Parliamentary office was close to ours, kindly came over to talk to me with his wife. However, when she realised I was not Jim's wife she gave me a look of disdain and quickly moved him along! I was not only embarrassed, but humiliated. I knew I had flushed bright red as she obviously thought Jim and I were having an affair. Jim was not a womaniser and I was certainly not interested in anything but a professional relationship in my working life.

I determined not to let this spoil my evening. Fortunately it was not long before we sat down to dinner, underneath the famous, if somewhat contentious, painting "Blue Poles." The Prime Minister gave a welcoming address and the rest of the evening passed pleasantly – the food was delicious and even the speeches were mostly entertaining.

I stayed in Canberra for the rest of the week and soon became familiar with our new setting. Without the rabbit warren of corridors of the old Parliament House it was easier to find your way around and the building was spacious, filled with light and surrounded by lovely courtyards with grass-edged pavers and trees. Tables and chairs were strategically placed – some in the shade for those few warm days and the rest in the direct sun. The staff cafeteria was a huge area with an improved selection of food – it was like eating in a restaurant every day. Although I didn't go to the bar, it was very well frequented in the evenings, by members and staffers alike. However, I couldn't help hankering just a little for the camaraderie which existed in the old Parliament House. Our grand new office suites were quite self-contained, so there was very little need to venture outside them. It was really only at the photocopier or cafeteria that people met up. There was less whispering in the corridors and I missed the gossip!

I went into Question Time one afternoon. The new gallery was very modern and the glass wall which cut you off from the politicians was so clear you felt you were actually in the Chamber. A couple of times I took papers into Jim whilst the House was in session – there were seats at the rear of the Chamber for politicians to converse with their staffers. Life in Canberra was an entirely different world – a mini-city with a feeling of surrealness, dislocated from real life.

Kareem

Kareem Hazif contacted me a couple of times whilst I waited to hear back from the Minister's office. He was always very polite and courteous, but obviously very distressed about the lack of information regarding his brother. The Minister's response, when it came, was not very helpful. Apparently the Australian Embassy in Cairo had spoken to Ramy's aunt and uncle when Kareem had first contacted them and they were unable to give much information. When they checked again, no further postcards had been received nor had Ramy made any contact with them. The airline's records showed that he had taken the flight to Abu Simbel but there was no record of him taking a flight back, nor of him leaving Egypt. The good news was that no-one matching Ramy's description had been found through the morgues or hospitals. The Minister's letter concluded by assuring the family the Embassy would continue to search for Ramy and advise of any developments.

I rang Kareem to let him know that the reply had arrived. He was anxious to receive it as soon as possible and wanted to pick it up on his way home from work.

"If you can wait until I can get there, I'll buy you coffee," he said.

I didn't normally become friendly with constituents on a personal level but I actually found him quite charming, so I decided to make an exception.

Kareem arrived around six. He was wearing a brown sports jacket and dark brown trousers with a white shirt that accentuated the olive colour of his skin. I handed him the Minister's letter. He read it slowly and put it carefully into his inside jacket pocket. His huge eyes searched my face inquiringly.

"What do I do now?" he asked.

"Well," I replied "I think you have to wait and see if the Embassy can find out any more information."

He looked thoughtful for a moment and then said:

"Come on, I'll buy you that coffee I promised you."

"There's really no need," I responded, feeling awful that I didn't have any better news for him.

"No, please, I would like to talk to you."

We walked around to the coffee shop and both ordered a cappuccino. Kareem sat quietly for a while, drinking his coffee.

"I must go to Egypt and search for my brother. My parents expect it of me," he said by way of explanation.

He sighed as if he was relieved to have made a decision that involved some action on his part. Then he smiled at me. "But enough of my problems. Tell me something of yourself."

I told him a little of my background and my job and we chatted amicably for a while. I was impressed by the way he listened intently as I spoke, how his eyes locked into mine and how he asked interested questions without probing too far into my personal life. I explained to him that both my parents had died at quite a young age and I had no brothers or sisters. I could see it upset him a little to know that I had no-one close as family was obviously very important to him. We sat there for a couple of hours before he paid the bill, saying:

"I have enjoyed your company, Anna. I would very much like to have dinner with you before I leave for Cairo. Can I ring you once I have made my bookings?"

'Yes, Kareem," I replied "I would like that."

A couple of days later the phone rang late in the afternoon and it was Kareem. I had found myself waiting for his call and it was nice to hear his voice.

"Anna," he said "are you free for dinner tomorrow night? I know it's short notice, but I am flying to Cairo Saturday morning and really want to see you again before I leave."

Not one for playing games I replied that I was indeed free this Friday.

"Do you like Italian food?" he asked.

"I like all food!" was my quick response. "Well, most food anyway" I added, remembering a visit to a Persian restaurant.

Kareem suggested a very nice local Italian restaurant and I said I would meet him there at seven thirty. I like to drive myself on dates until I know someone really well –it gives me a quick out if I need one and keeps my home address unknown!

When I arrived on Friday Kareem was already there waiting for me. I like people to be on time so that was another big tick in his favour! It turned out to be a great night – the food was excellent, the wine Kareem chose was really good and he was fun to be with. I had a wonderful evening and was really sorry when we finished our coffee. It was only then that Kareem mentioned Ramy again and his trip to Egypt the next day. He showed me a photo of his brother standing by a lake – a younger looking Kareem with the same eyes and eyelashes but with a more outgoing stance and a beautiful smile.

"He is very confident," Kareem explained. "He likes new challenges and is very athletic. I have taken some leave. I hope I can find Ramy. Apparently his credit card and bank account have not been accessed."

"Where are you going to start your search?" I asked him.

"I will go and see our aunt and uncle in Cairo first. I doubt that there is anything they can tell me that they haven't already told the Embassy. However I should go and see them as I know they are very worried too. Then I will fly up to Abu Simbel – that is where Ramy was going when he left Cairo. From there.....who knows? I will ask a lot of questions and see where they lead me.

Can I see you again when I get back?" he asked. I nodded my agreement.

Kareem saw me to my car and his lips brushed my cheek as he said goodbye. I could tell he was keen to see me again but that his mind was already turning to the task ahead of him.

"Be careful and good luck – I hope you find Ramy quickly and that he is okay.... just having too good a time to contact anyone!"

It was only ten days before I heard from Kareem again. I had just arrived home from work when the phone rang.

"It's me," he said "Kareem. I'm back in Australia. I haven't found Ramy – I had to come home, my father has had a heart attack. I'm sure it's the stress and worry about Ramy. I saw him last night and he was so disappointed I hadn't found him. He has made me promise to keep searching until I track him down."

"I'm so sorry Kareem - about Ramy and your father. How are you? How was Egypt?" I added "I haven't heard any more from Foreign Affairs unfortunately."

"I'm fine. I'm not really surprised you haven't heard from Foreign Affairs. Can we have dinner?" he asked. "Then I can tell you all about my trip."

We agreed to meet the next evening at the same restaurant as before. All day at work I found myself thinking about the evening ahead and had to admit the prospect of seeing Kareem again excited me.

I arrived just as Kareem was getting out of his car. He came over and hugged me warmly.

"It's so good to see you again," he said simply.

"How is your father" I asked.

"He's much better," Kareem replied. "They're talking about him coming home tomorrow."

Over our meal Kareem told me of his efforts to locate Ramy.

"First I went to see our uncle and aunt but they had still not received any message from Ramy. They feel responsible for him, you know – he had been their guest and had disappeared. I tried to reassure them that it was Ramy's decision to leave their home and they should not feel that way. After staying the night I then booked myself on a flight to Abu Simbel. The place is amazing, I wish you could have been with me to experience it. I had no idea Abu Simbel would be so imposing. The statues are huge and they are in the middle of nowhere. They just rise out of the hillside and are so beautifully carved out of the rock.

Anyway, after wandering around for a while I booked into a hotel and started showing the photo of Ramy around to the tour guides and the local shops, but to no avail. I decided to go back to the temples for the light show that evening. I took the photo with me and asked the guides on duty that night but no-one remembered him. The show itself was well worth seeing – the statues were lit up in different coloured lights using lasers which flashed this way and that and a recorded voice boomed out across the stillness of the night telling the story of Abu Simbel.

The next day I had a breakthrough. A

woman in one of the shops remembered seeing my brother because of his funny accent and the fact that he was with a very attractive Egyptian woman. Apparently she bought a very expensive handbag. However there was nothing more that she could tell me other than that they had been there. Then a waitress at the resort remembered that Ramy had spent a night there with the Egyptian woman. He had asked her about catching a boat to Aswan. I thought I'm finally making some progress.

I spent all of the next day showing photos to staff on the boats but with no result. No-one remembered seeing Ramy. But there are many tour boats so I decided to join one going down the Nile to Aswan. Perhaps someone there would remember him. It was a very interesting trip but I was anxious to get to Aswan to resume my search. Once we arrived I walked around the other boats talking to staff and showing the photo of Ramy. However, no-one there remembered seeing him either. I stayed in Aswan and spent three days going through the bazaars, talking to the drivers of the horse-drawn cabs, going into hotels, trying to find someone who remembered seeing him. I couldn't find anyone who did. I thought if only I had a photo of the woman, maybe they would remember the two of them together.

Anyway, I decided to move on to Luxor. One of the locals had his own boat and took me down there early in the morning. He suggested I go to see his brother, Jahi, who had a souvenir shop in the bazaar near the port. He is well known in Luxor and knew a lot of the comings and goings of the town. So I went to see Jahi. He didn't recognise my brother from the photo but he promised to make some inquiries for me. I gave him a copy of the photo and booked into a hotel. I spent the rest of the day talking to anyone I thought might be able to help but all to no avail.

The next morning Jahi turned up at my hotel. "I have some news for you" he said proudly. He told me that his inquiries around Luxor had not met with any success. However, that evening he went to dinner at his cousin's house and he was telling him about Ramy and the attractive Egyptian girl. His cousin became quite excited and said a very attractive girl had stayed in his hotel for a couple of nights with an Australian-sounding man. He grabbed the photo from me and said "Yes, yes, that is him." He said the couple had a row on the second night and the Australian stormed out. However, he came back soon after and they left together the next day, although he didn't know where they were heading.

It was then I made a call home, to be told my father was in hospital, so I came back to Australia as quickly as I could."

"Where are you going to look next?" I asked him.

"I will have to go back to Luxor and take it up again from there. I need to talk to the cousin who owned the hotel where they stayed. But first I need to make sure my father is home and well again. My mother needs my support right now. Enough of all this though, I want to know what you have been doing in my absence."

The rest of the evening passed quickly and pleasantly. I was happy to discover I was still attracted to Kareem and that I wanted to see him again. I had wondered if my initial interest would have waned, as it sometimes does after a couple of dates, or that Kareem would have decided I wasn't so interesting after all! After dinner Kareem walked me to my car. As he opened the door he kissed me on the cheek. I agreed he could pick me up from home the next night and we would go for a pizza.

"Did your father come home today?" I asked as I got into his car the following night.
"Yes, he did," Kareem replied. "He was very pleased to be back in his favourite chair and my mother is fussing around him like an old hen. He wants to meet this woman who is taking me away from him in the evenings. They would like you to come for dinner on the week-end."
So Saturday night Kareem picked me up and took me around to his parents' home. It was a two-storey house in a good area and decorated in very lavish style, with many pieces of furniture I would describe as Egyptian. Mrs Hazif was very welcoming and

put me at ease straight away and Kareem's father, still pale and drawn, was interested in my job. I was able to tell him a couple of funny stories from work and made him laugh. We then sat down to roast lamb, which was a relief, as I wasn't sure if I would like Egyptian food. It was a relaxed evening but after coffee I could see Kareem's dad was looking very tired so I made a move to leave and Kareem drove me home.

This time he came in for a nightcap. I poured him a scotch and myself a Baileys and we sat on the lounge together for a while listening to Elvis. When Kareem stood up and offered me his hand to dance I felt very much at home in his arms.

Well, I'm sure I don't need to tell you any more – you know what happened next – right?

Search for Ramy

Kareem left around two in the morning and I slept in the next morning until about eight o'clock. 'Thank goodness it's Saturday', I thought, as I lay in bed thinking about the previous night. 'Who wants to go to work after such a night?'

The phone rang whilst I was still lying there. It was Kareem.

"Good morning," he said "how are you this morning"?

"I'm fine – how about you?" I responded.

"Oh, very good," he said" I had the most wonderful evening with a wonderful woman." He laughed. "I was wondering if I can see you later today?"

Unfortunately, I had already booked a hair appointment for the morning and was meeting a girlfriend in the afternoon for a movie and dinner. Reluctantly I said I couldn't make it.

"What about Sunday?" I inquired.

"You have a date," said Kareem. "I'll pick you up at eleven and we'll spend the day together."

Sunday was a glorious day. We drove down to Cronulla and caught the ferry across to Bundeena. There were quite a few people on the beach and children playing in the water. We bought fish and chips and sat on the pier watching them. Then we walked the length of Jibbon Beach and I took Kareem along the path around the headland to see the aboriginal carvings. He was suitably impressed.

"Look, this one looks like a whale," he exclaimed "and this one is a turtle."

"Isn't it amazing?" I said "To think they have survived for so many years and yet they are so close to the city and anyone can stroll along here and see them."

It was low tide so we went back along the rocks, scrambling to beat the odd wave and enjoying the sea breeze. The bay was full of small boats anchored close to the shore. Children swam in the sea, jumping off their boats and clambering back up the ladders at great speed to do it all again. Little children busied themselves on the sand, making sandcastles or digging moats ready for the sea to fill them. Everyone was relaxed and happy, enjoying their day out by the water. On our trip back on the ferry the sea was sparkling like diamonds as the sun hit the waves and the little ferry rose and fell with the swell. Kareem sat with his arm around me and I had never been happier.

We bought some Thai food on the way in and Kareem stayed until late. I was curious as to why he was still living at home with his parents and asked him about it.

"Ah, well," he said "it has not always been so. I was married for three years but it didn't work out. I went home to lick my wounds but then I realised my father was not really up to doing the garden or other maintenance so I stayed on. Just laziness really – I could live nearby and still do these things. Mum's cooking of course is a key factor in all of this!"

We talked until well into the night until Kareem said "It's time to get you to bed."

"I thought you'd never ask!" I responded.

Over the next few days I saw Kareem nearly every night. In the meantime, he checked again with the Embassy in Cairo, inquired from the Bank as to whether Ramy's credit card or account had been used and continued to watch over his father. He had returned to work at his job as an accountant in a large practice in the City, conserving his leave for another trip to Egypt once his father was stable.

Things were getting very interesting in Canberra at this time too. I usually spoke to Colleen a couple of times a day and she told me the word was out that there was to be a Labor leadership spill. The polls had indicated that the public would not accept another term under Labor with Bob Hawke as the PM. It was planned to ditch Hawke and replace him with Paul Keating. By promoting the Leader rather than the Party it was thought that the electorate would go for this new fresh look from the same tired old Party.

There was always a huge buzz in Parliament house when a leadership spill was about to take place. The rumours were rife for days beforehand and everyone eagerly awaited the result. There was much whispering in corners in the corridors and offices and Jim would walk around as if he didn't have any idea that anything was going on. The media would comment on it day and night and report on the numbers believed to be supporting each candidate. Even Jim's wife would be on the phone to see if we had heard any further news. The so-called Numbers Man of the party would be very busy ringing each of the MPs and Senators to see which way they were going to vote at the spill. Part of me wished I was down there amongst the action whilst the other part of me wanted to stay in Sydney to be close to Kareem.

Paul Keating was successful in taking the reins from Bob Hawke in December 1991, just as the rumour mill had said he would be.

Later that week I received a phone call from Kareem at work.

"It's my father," he said obviously extremely upset. "He had another heart attack during the night and my mother found him dead beside her in the morning. She is very upset she didn't hear anything."

"Oh Kareem, I'm so sorry," I responded. "Please tell your mother I'm thinking of her. If there's anything I can do....."

"I have to arrange the funeral. I hope you understand I have a lot to do and I may not be able to see you for a few days."

"Yes, of course," I replied. "If I can help in any way, please let me know."

I felt so sorry for Kareem and his mother. Mr Hazif had seemed to be recovering so well and it was a bolt out of the blue for them.

I went to the funeral. It was a small, private service at the local crematorium and afterwards we gathered at the house. It was very sad – no celebration of life – just family and close friends mourning the loss of a loved one. I felt honoured to be included in this small number and to have had the opportunity to have met Kareem's father.

A couple of weeks later, over dinner at my place, Kareem announced it was time for him to resume his search for Ramy.

"My mother has lost her husband and her son is still missing, I must go and find him" he said simply.

I made an instant decision.

"I'll come with you. I have a few weeks' leave accumulated – you know how it is, there is never a good time in politics to take it. I want to help you find Ramy."

I knew from the look in Kareem's eyes that he was pleased.

"It will be hard work," he said, "not much of a holiday, but it will be great to have you with me."

Two days later we were on the flight to Cairo. What a fascinating city! The traffic was frenetic – the taxi we took from the airport weaved in and out of lanes with a blast of his horn. As everyone else was using their horn, the result to my unaccustomed ears and eyes seemed chaotic and dangerous.

Kareem had booked us into the Marriott Hotel – a beautiful hotel which was once a small palace. It was like an oasis in the middle of this busy city, the new accommodation wing being very sympathetic to the original structure. It had huge colonnades and underneath, along the length of it, were tables with green umbrellas surrounded by lovely gardens and on the level below a magnificent swimming pool. The pool went under an arch at one end and into the shade. The majority of it however was in the sun, with tiered gardens overlooking it. We were to have one night of luxury before heading for Luxor and we made the most of it! We swam in the pool, ate dinner in the gardens lit with fairy lights, luxuriated in the huge bed and had a hearty breakfast before heading off the next day.

Before we took the flight to Luxor we went to see Kareem's uncle and aunt. They made us very welcome and I could understand how Ramy would have spent a very pleasant month in their company. Their house had a very peaceful inner courtyard which was like an oasis from the traffic and noise of the city. Kareem told them in detail about his progress on his previous visit and they agreed they would be the contact point for Kareem and his mother. Naturally, Kareem was anxious about leaving his mother alone so soon after his father died and he wanted to make sure she knew he was okay. We had coffee with them and some delicious Egyptian cakes, before heading off to the airport.

I liked Luxor better than Cairo – it's not as chaotic. We went to the hotel of Jahi's cousin, Hamadi. He was dressed in western clothes and spoke reasonably good English. He appeared to be in his thirties, average looking and with short black hair. Kareem introduced himself and Hamadi was pleased to meet him.

"Your brother," he said "he stayed here with the attractive Egyptian lady. Have you found him yet?"

"No," replied Kareem, "we are here to search for him. Do you have a room for us?"

"Of course" said Hamadi "I give you my best room. Go and make yourselves comfortable and after we will talk."

It was not the Marriott but it was clean and comfortable and looked out on to the street. The main bazaar was just around the corner. We went downstairs and Hamadi had coffee waiting for us in the lounge.

"I can't tell you very much," said Hamadi apologetically. "They stayed the night – they had a big row and your brother walked out but he came back after a couple of hours and then they left the next day. The lady, she came from a good family. She had beautiful jewellery and she conducted herself like a lady. That's all I know – I don't know where they were going. I have asked around the bazaar but no-one can tell me anything. I suggest you try some of the tour operators. Maybe someone will remember something."

We spent the rest of the afternoon showing

Ramy's photo around but to no avail. It was very hot and sticky – I was glad when Kareem finally said "Let's call it a day. We'll go back to the hotel and take a shower and then go somewhere for a drink."

I was in the shower – letting the tepid water cool my body – when Kareem shouted out:

"I'll be back in a minute – there's a call for me in reception."

He returned as I came out of the bathroom.

"That was my uncle. Someone has contacted my mother," he explained. "They say they have Ramy and want two hundred and fifty thousand Australian dollars. She told them I am in Egypt and we will get the money. She has already arranged a mortgage on the house and will wire it via Western Union tomorrow or the next day. She has also spoken to the police and they will monitor the next call, although how it will help from Sydney I don't know."

I put my arms around him and he laid his head on my shoulder.

"Thank goodness he is alive and will soon be able to come home with us" he said.

We went out for that cold drink. We found a café overlooking the Nile and sat into the evening and had dinner there. Neither of us was very interested in what we were eating. I couldn't help wondering why it had taken so long to get the ransom call. How long had Ramy been missing now? It was over two months. Normally you would expect to get the ransom call within a day or two. Or maybe he hadn't been missing all that time but had just been having a fun with his new girlfriend and then something had gone wrong. Something didn't seem quite right though. I tried to bring this up but Kareem was just too excited at the thought of rescuing his brother to fully take in what I was saying.

"Maybe he was trying to get Ramy to find the money," he reasoned. "Or maybe Ramy wasn't telling them who he was or where his family lived. He can be very stubborn when he wants to be."

It occurred to me that no-one is going to be very stubborn if their life is being threatened, but I kept the thought to myself – it didn't seem to be the right moment to share it.

The Ransom

Two days later Kareem and I went to Western Union and collected the money. I had begged Kareem to go to the local police but the kidnappers had insisted that there be no police involved if we wanted to see Ramy alive.

"Besides," Kareem pointed out "the local police are often very corrupt and they may relieve me of the money before I can pay the ransom!"

I was very jumpy as we walked back from the Western Union office to the hotel with the equivalent of two hundred and fifty thousand Australian dollars in a bag!

Kareem rang his uncle. The kidnappers had contacted Kareem's mother again and told him to be at the Temple of Luxor at eight fifteen the next day with the money. He was, of course, to go alone and to proceed towards the back of the Temple. He would see his brother behind one of the columns and a man in traditional clothing would take the bag with the money in exchange for Ramy. Unfortunately, the Australian police told his mother, the call was not long enough for it to be traced.

I was so nervous as Kareem set off. I begged him to let me go with him – at least as far as the Temple entrance, but he was adamant he would not jeopardise his brother's life by taking any chances.

By half past ten I was very anxious. He

should have been back by now – where was he? Eleven o'clock came and went and by now I was pacing the small reception area. Surely it couldn't take that long. Even if Ramy was ill and they had gone straight to the hospital, I would have expected a call from Kareem by now. I forced myself to be calm. There would be a very good reason – maybe there was a bomb threat and the Temple had opened late. Maybe Ramy was so ill Kareem had taken him straight to a hospital and hadn't thought to ring me. By mid-afternoon I could contain my fears no longer. I put a call through to Kareem's uncle. He wasn't there, of course, he was at work. His wife said she would contact him and get him to ring me straight back. More waiting. But within fifteen minutes his Uncle was on the phone.

"Something must be wrong Anna," he said. "I have a bad feeling. Wait another hour and then go to the police."

That hour was the longest of my life. I kept going over and over Kareem's last words. "I will take a taxi to the Temple and find my brother. We will come back in a taxi and ring my mother. Then we will go out and have a big celebratory lunch. I will not be long."

At four o'clock I went downstairs again. Hamadi was at Reception. I told him what had happened and he straight away said he would take me to the police station - I would probably need an interpreter. I was very glad of his company; by now I was starting to feel very much alone. The police station was about ten minutes away in the taxi and Hamadi pushed through the throng of people waiting to talk to someone. He said something to the policeman on the desk and in a couple of minutes we were ushered into a room. The policeman who seemed to be in charge came in to talk to us. Hamadi explained that my friend's brother had been kidnapped and my friend had gone to pay the ransom money and not returned. Through Hamadi I told him what had happened to date. He spoke some English but he was very hard to understand and I was glad of Hamadi's help.

"We will look into it," he assured me and then we were back out in the sunshine and the heat and on our way back to the hotel.

The rest of that day and the next day I waited at the hotel, not wanting to be absent if Kareem turned up and not wanting to miss any contact from the police. In the meantime I put a call through to the Australian Embassy and arranged an appointment for Thursday. It couldn't come quick enough.

Next morning Hamadi arranged a taxi for me from the hotel to Luxor Temple. Hamadi had warned me not to go out on the street on my own and not to catch a taxi off the street. "Make sure you get the hotel to book you a taxi and then wherever you go get them to call you one back to the hotel. Just like Cairo, it is not safe to for tourists, especially women on their own." I wanted to see where Kareem had disappeared. I knew I wasn't going to find him there but I needed to see where he had gone to meet his brother's kidnappers, believing he would be returning with Ramy. I wanted, I suppose, to feel closer to him, to look for clues, just to see if there was anything that would give me an idea as to what had happened. I had a photo of the two of us taken in Aswan and I showed it at the ticket office and to the guards, but no-one remembered seeing Kareem. Seeing the throng of people swarming over the temple, I wasn't really surprised.

The Temple itself was amazing – even though I was not there to sightsee I could not help but be impressed by its size and beauty. Unlike Greece or Italy, where many of the ruins are incomplete and leave an enormous amount to your imagination, in Egypt they are very well preserved and large parts of them are intact. The entrance is flanked by two large statues of Pharaohs (over fifteen metres high) and I walked through an avenue lined with huge engraved columns and statues. I saw the sitting Ramses II statue, huge and imposing and the red granite obelisk, covered in carvings and towering against the blue sky. Covering two hundred and sixty square metres in length the Temple of Luxor is truly breathtaking. I took in the avenue of sphinxes with rams' heads which apparently become human heads as you approach the Temple of Karnak about three kilometres further on. For a while I was totally entranced by the height and size of these amazing images, still in such wonderful original condition. It was fascinating to see part of a way of life from so many years ago. The Temple weaved a sort of magic and for the first time since Kareem went missing I was able to forget the pain and the stress of this horrible ordeal. However, eventually my mind pulled itself out of this make-believe world and back to the present.

I wandered amongst the columns and imagined where I thought the exchange would have taken place. I passed another guard and showed him the photo of Kareem, but he just shook his head. I wasn't sure how much English he understood but he obviously didn't recognise the photo. Eventually, hot, tired and exhausted, I gave up and returned to the hotel.

Late that afternoon I flew back to Cairo, to the sanctuary of the Marriott. I couldn't help but remember where Kareem and I had sat and enjoyed drinks over-looking the gardens, how we swam in the pool before breakfast and ate dinner in the garden under the stars.

My appointment was with a John Turner at ten o'clock the next day and I caught a taxi from the hotel. I liked John as soon as I met him. A typical tanned, blue-eyed Aussie he was very friendly and easy to talk to. He had a diplomat's voice, very well-spoken - he could have had a job with the ABC. Apparently he had been with Foreign Affairs all his life and had been in Egypt for nearly two years. He didn't try to fob me off but listened whilst I told him about Kareem's meeting with the kidnappers and how he hadn't returned. He had the file on Ramy in front of him and was familiar with the actions taken to try and trace him. John promised to make some further inquiries and get back to me. I told him I was returning to the hotel at Luxor, I felt comfortable there and had Hamadi to help me as an interpreter. Also it was a lot cheaper than the Marriott! Before I left he gave me access to the phone to ring Jim. I didn't think I'd have much chance of catching him - when Parliament was not sitting he was either at a meeting or attending an opening or other electorate event. However, my luck was in and I was able to fill him in on what had happened.

"I'm so sorry," he said. "I'll contact the Ambassador myself and ask him to give you every assistance. If I can help in any way let me know, and don't worry about work."

I replaced the phone and said goodbye to John. His blue eyes looked deeply into mine and I felt reassured that he would do everything in his power to help me.

I flew back to Luxor that afternoon and Hamadi greeted me warmly. But what was I to do now? I couldn't just sit around the hotel, but it didn't make sense to be in Cairo. I lay awake most of the night, reliving the events of the past few days and trying to make some sense of it all. Why had the kidnappers waited so long to make contact and where was Kareem? Had they kidnapped him too? Had he been killed? Was Ramy still alive or already dead when they made the ransom call? I resolved to stay put for a couple of days and wait and see if the Embassy could find anything out for me or (a long shot I knew) maybe Kareem would suddenly turn up at the hotel. In the meantime, tomorrow I would go and see the Temple of Karnak – there is plenty to see in Egypt to pass the time. Of one thing I was sure - I would go mad if I just sat around the hotel waiting!

When I awoke it was late – I had finally dropped off to sleep and made up for it the next morning. After breakfast I found Hamadi and told him I was going to Karnak and asked him to call me a taxi.

"I'll come with you," he said. "I need a break and I can show you around."

Karnak was also amazing. Hamadi was a good guide – he gave me information on the Temple without going overboard as they tend to do on a tour.

"Although badly ruined" he explained "no site in Egypt is more impressive than Karnak. It is the largest temple complex ever built by man. It is actually three temples, enclosed by these enormous brick walls. Only the largest, Amun-Re is open to the public. Luxor Temple, which you saw the other day, is outside these enclosed walls, joined to Karnak by the avenues of the sphinxes."

I found myself marvelling again at the

incredible size and accuracy of the statues and columns. All those years ago, man had been able to make such huge, perfect and beautiful works of art that we were still enjoying today. Everywhere you looked there were hieroglyphics depicting stories – Ramses II, the Queen Nefertari with her servants bearing gifts of food and wine, depictions of fighting with dying enemies surrounding the King, Gods Horus, Isis, Rae all featured with offerings of servants and food. Hamadi gave me a short history on each of the main players in these scenes in front of me. It was fascinating and I found myself drawn into the mystery of this world of long ago. To think that these people had walked amongst these same columns all those years before! They had worked, loved, had families and lost loved ones, no doubt had mortgages and debts, just as we do today. And yet this huge, strong civilisation was no more. It was very humbling and made me realise just how unimportant we are in the general scheme of things.

We returned to the hotel and I had a late lunch before settling into a sunlounge in the leafy courtyard with a book. Try as I might though, I couldn't concentrate. I re-read the first page three times before giving up and falling into a light sleep in which I was being chased by people with rams' faces! I was relieved then when Hamadi came and woke me.

"Come quickly" he said 'The Australian Embassy is on the phone for you."

It was John Turner. "Sorry to get your hopes up" he said. "I don't have any news but I just wanted to let you know I am working on it. How are you today?"

I said I was fine. His voice was friendly and warm and I knew from his tone that he didn't ring all his compatriots to give such an update. It was nice to hear from someone who seemed to care though and made me feel less alone in this country so alien to me.

"Look," he said "I was thinking I might fly up there and have a look around the Temple of Luxor where the ransom exchange was to take place. I can ask a few questions and maybe someone will remember something. If I come up tomorrow will you come out to the Temple with me?"

I explained that I had already been out there but none of the guards seemed to remember seeing anything.

"It will be easier for me as I speak some Egyptian" he pointed out. "It's worth a try isn't it?"

I readily agreed that anything was worth a try and at least I would be doing something other than sitting around. He arranged to pick me up at the hotel at one o'clock.

I was already waiting outside the hotel when John pulled up in a taxi at the designated time the next day.

"Jump in," he said and gave me a warm smile. "Let's go and see what we can find out."

The Temple of Luxor was just as impressive on my second visit. I think I took more in too because on the first occasion I was concentrating so hard on trying to find out something about Kareem's disappearance. John was a good guide and pointed out the most important aspects of the Temple. He explained that whilst Amenophis III built most of the complex, the first courtyard, including the statues of the seated pharaohs and the obelisks at the entrance was the work of Ramses II. "No other city had so many obelisks and colossi made from a single stone" John told me. It was nice to be with an Australian again, to talk easily without the language or accent restraints. I suddenly became overwhelmingly homesick.

'What was I doing here, so far from home?' I thought for a moment. Then I thought of Kareem and our time together and I reproached myself for even thinking this.

We made our way to the columns where Kareem was to have met with the kidnappers. John saw a guard in his black garb.

"Here, give me the photo of Kareem," he said. He took it over to the guard and asked him something in Egyptian. He was a different man from the one I had tried to speak to on my first visit. They exchanged a few words and he looked intently at the photo. He nodded his head and became very garrulous. John came back to me smiling.

"He said there was a bit of an incident that morning. He heard a cry and came around the corner in time to see a man running away with a bag and another man lying on the ground. He went over to assist him but he jumped up and chased off after the other man. That was all he knew and he was the closest to the scene. But at least it's something" John added. "We know the kidnappers took the money, that obviously they didn't relinquish his brother and that Kareem was alive and well at that point."

John talked to the other guards but no-one else remembered seeing Kareem. One of them confirmed that there was an incident that day but said it was all over by the time he arrived.

We returned to my hotel and I invited John for a cold drink at the bar. We talked easily until it was time for him to catch his return flight to Cairo. He wanted to speak of Australia and what was happening in the political scene. He said he was very homesick and was hoping his next posting would be back in Australia – preferably in Canberra. Then all too soon it was time for him to go and he left promising to contact me as soon as he had any news.

Kareem's Disappearance

It was a couple of days later when John Turner rang to say there had been a report to the police in Cairo of a husband and daughter going missing. The daughter's description matched that of Ramy's girlfriend, so John was going to interview the mother himself that morning. He had asked her to bring in a photo and he said he would ring me as soon as he had spoken with her.

It was an anxious couple of hours before he called back. I drank numerous cups of coffee and paced the hotel lobby. When he rang he confirmed that it was indeed the same woman seen with Ramy.

"Her name is Yasmeen and I asked the mother if she would be willing to talk to you. She said she would do anything to find her husband and daughter. Why don't you get yourself on a flight to Cairo?"

I didn't need telling twice. That afternoon I was back in Cairo, with the photo of Yasmeen and Ramy. I took a taxi straight to the shop, which was underneath their home. Mrs Ahmose welcomed me, saying "Please, call me Waleed." Not very tall and slightly overweight, she was still a very beautiful woman and I thought what a stunner she would have been in her youth. She wore a pair of beautifully tailored slacks and a very decorative black top with a black peacock picked out in green sequins. Her long fingernails were painted a very dark red which matched her lipstick perfectly and were covered in expensive looking rings.

"Come, meet my sons Omar and Pili." Two very good looking young men in their early twenties greeted me. It was obviously not just their sister who had inherited their mother's good looks.

John had already explained my situation to Mrs Ahmose and she was happy to talk to me. Over a cup of tea I filled her in as best I could on Kareem's disappearance. She nodded and then told me about her husband's disappearance.

"He received a phone call," she explained "saying that Yasmeen was being held captive and that he had to go to the Valley of the Queens to get her back. He was not supposed to tell anyone, especially not the police. He only told me because he knew I would worry if he was gone too long and that I would then call the police. He told me not to tell anyone, not even our boys."

"But what did they want in exchange for Yasmeen?" I asked her.

"He didn't tell me," she replied. "He just said not to worry, everything would be alright – he would take care of everything. When they didn't return the next night, nor the next, I was worried sick. I told the boys what had happened and they wanted to go up to the Valley of the Queens but I forbade them to. I said I needed their support here and they should keep the shop running so if anyone was watching us they would not be suspicious.

After a week had passed I went to the police – what else could I do? For all I know, I will never see either of them again."

At this she started weeping but I could see there were few tears left – Mrs Ahmose had obviously already done a lot of crying over the past few weeks.

"The police have found nothing," Mrs Ahmose continued after a couple of minutes. "There have been no reports of any unidentified bodies, they have contacted the ticket office at the Valley of the Queens and they had seen nothing suspicious. I don't even know if my husband made it there. Why would they want to meet him there? It doesn't make any sense to me. We are quite well off but we are not super rich. If they wanted money, why didn't they tell Masud to take the money with him? My husband takes care of all our financial matters, but after we had heard nothing from the police I spoke to the Bank and he has not withdrawn any large sum of money. In fact he has not withdrawn any money since he left – the Bank has undertaken to contact me immediately if the accounts are activated."

Omar interrupted us at this point.

"It is time we went to look for them ourselves," he told his mother. "We cannot just sit around like this, day after day, wondering what has happened to them. We have waited long enough – it is time for Pili and me to go and search for them."

Mrs Ahmose became very upset then.

"Isn't it enough that my husband and only daughter are missing? You want me to be left alone to run the shop and worry about what is happening to you as well as to them? You want me to end up childless?" she remonstrated.

I interrupted her.

"I will keep looking for them," I assured the boys. "The police are looking and the Australian Embassy is trying to find Ramy and Kareem. You really are better off looking after the shop and your mother. You need to be here in case there is any contact from your father or sister."

This seemed to appease them but it was clear they were anxious to do something practical to find Yasmeen and Mr Ahmose.

"Tomorrow is Sunday," I said to them. "Why don't you drive me out to the Valley of the Queens where your father was to meet with them and we will see if there are any clues there to their disappearance."

This suggestion seemed to be satisfactory to everyone. I had intended to return to Luxor that night so I hadn't booked any accommodation. I asked Mrs Ahmose if there was a small hotel nearby where I might stay, but she insisted that I sleep in Yasmeen's old room.

"It will be nice to have some female company," she said as I helped her change the sheets. "Yasmeen is a good daughter, she comes as regularly as she can with her job and often stays overnight."

Over dinner I also learned a bit about Mr Ahmose and Yasmeen. It seemed both were quite worldly wise and not the types to be easily duped. Mrs Ahmose was very proud of her daughter, who she said was clever and hard-working.

"She loves the antiques," she told me. "I know she would love to work in the shop but her father thinks it is a man's world. Perhaps one day she will open her own shop."

This of course brought more tears as she contemplated the possibility that Yasmeen would not be returning home. We spent the rest of the evening going over possible scenarios for their disappearance. Mr Ahmose was highly regarded in the community and well-known in the antique business. I asked Mrs Ahmose if she thought her husband might have come across a rare antique so valuable that someone would kidnap Yasmeen and hold her for ransom.

"If he had such a valuable piece, I am sure he would have mentioned it to me," she replied.

Obviously they were a devoted couple, although clearly Mr Ahmose made all the decisions in the family and his wife tended to the home, as was their traditional custom.

The next morning we were all up early and after a very filling breakfast Omar, Pili and I set off for the Valley of the Queens. Mrs Ahmose stood at the door waving to us and dabbing her eyes with her handkerchief. Omar did the driving and he and Pili said very little on the way, both caught up in their private thoughts and their hopes of finding something that would lead us to their father and sister. Occasionally they would make a comment about the road or another driver. It seemed Omar, being the eldest, was more confident than his brother but I had the feeling that Pili was perhaps the smarter of the two. Both were very good looking and wore designer jeans and open-necked shirts. Both had dark, flashing eyes that took in everything around them. Neither were very tall but they walked with an air of confidence that added height. Their manners were impeccable and I felt very comfortable with them. I also spent much of the journey lost in thought, hoping against hope that we might find Ramy and that Kareem would somehow be with him.

We parked at Queen Hatshepsut's tomb. We took the photo of Ramy and Yasmeen over to the guards and asked them if they had seen them. They all replied in the negative. Pili also showed them a photo of his father, but this brought the same response.

We wandered around the tomb. Pili told me that Queen Hatshepsut had ruled for twenty-two years, bringing Egypt peace and prosperity. When her husband, King Thutmosis II died, she became co-regent with her twelve-year old stepson, Thutmosis III. As he approached manhood she declared herself a Pharaoh and insisted on being depicted as a man by adding a beard to her statues, as kings were considered to be demi-gods.

"It is generally believed," he concluded "that it was Thutmosis III who had her face damaged or removed wherever possible after her death."

We started the trek up the hillside, not knowing what we were looking for or where we should look. There were little caves dotted around everywhere in the hills, many of which held the bodies of the working class. We tried calling out, but although our voices echoed around the hills, there was no answering call. The going was tough and after walking around for a couple of hours we decided this course of action was hopeless. If Mr Ahmose had been here, he was either long gone, or dead and buried in one of the caves.

Pili went to speak again to one of the guards to see if there was a road that went behind the tomb. From the gesturing and pointing it seemed that there was. Pili came back to the car, his brow and shirt damp from sweat and confirmed that we could pick up a track back from where we had turned off to the tomb. The track was only dirt and we bumped and bounced along it for about half an hour. There was nothing to see other than the barren hills and more caves. We stopped and walked over to a hill with several caves and peered inside them, but there was nothing to be seen. We called their names but our voices echoed back to us and there was no reply. Soon the sun was starting to set and we had to admit defeat and call it a day.

Omar and Pili dropped me off at Hamadi's

hotel. They stayed for a cold drink and then set off for the return trip to Cairo. I promised to keep digging and to let them know if I had any news.

Hamadi was keen to know what we had been up to and was not surprised that our search in the Valley of the Queen's had not produced any results.

"It is quite a wild and barren area," he told me. "Over the hill from Queen Hatshepsut's tomb there are many ravines and gulleys where a man could hide or be hidden. Very few people venture out into that part of the country."

The next morning I called around to the Police Station but the news was always the same.

"We have no further leads on Kareem's disappearance," the Sergeant told me. He was large and sweaty and appeared not to have very much interest in this case.

"As soon as we hear something we will let you know," he said, walking me to the door.

In other words – don't call us, we'll call you.

I phoned through to John at the Australian Embassy. It was nice to hear his cheerful voice again. I filled him in on my meeting with Mrs Ahmose and my trip to the Valley of the Queens with her sons and my visit to the Police Station. He was pleased that I had met with the family but not surprised that we had found nothing at the Valley of the Queens.

"Unfortunately, I too have no news at this stage," he said. "They seem to have just disappeared into thin air. I had hoped Mrs Ahmose might have told you something she hasn't told me – I have the feeling she is holding something back."

We talked a bit about Australia and what was happening there and then I hung up, promising to call in and see John next time I was in Cairo.

Hamadi found me some time later, sitting in the bar with a coke, staring into space. My mind was too tired to think and I was at a loss as to what to do next.

"Something will happen soon Anna, I feel sure of it," he said, trying to console me. "Many people are looking for them – it can't be long before someone sees something."

I went to bed early that night, emotional and exhausted. What was I doing here, in a land I didn't understand, looking for someone I had only known for a few weeks? I eventually fell asleep, only to dream I was being chased by a man carrying a huge 'Paul Hogan' knife. Then I fell into a deep hole and I was falling, falling......

When I awoke the next morning the sun had been up for quite a while but I felt lethargic and tired and not at all refreshed. Whilst I was having breakfast Hamadi came to tell me there was a call for me. It was Mrs Ahmose.

"Anna, my dear," she said. "It's Waleed. I have something I must tell you. Can you come to see me again? I'm sorry to ask you this but I do not want to tell you over the phone in case someone is listening. You can stay overnight in Yasmeen's room again."

I quickly agreed that I would fly to Cairo as soon as I could get a flight. I managed to get one later that morning and rang John to tell him I would be in Cairo that day and would ring him once I knew what it was Waleed wanted to tell me.

The Secret

I sat back in my seat as the plane took off and calculated how much I had spent on airfares since Kareem had disappeared. My meagre holiday money would soon be spent and I would have to think about returning to work – not only because of finances but because I couldn't expect Jim to manage without me much longer, especially when I was not making any headway.

Mrs Ahmose made me very welcome when I arrived. She had tea and cakes waiting for us in the lounge. Again she told me to call her by her first name, Waleed. Omar and Pili were nowhere to be seen – I gathered they were downstairs working in the shop.

"What is it you want to tell me?" I asked, wanting to find out as quickly as possible.

"There is something I should have told you before, but my husband made me promise never to tell anyone. In fact I had forgotten all about it, it was so many years ago. It was only when Omar asked me if I knew where the golden collar and jewelled dagger were that I remembered. It seems they are missing. I think Masud took them with him and that is what reminded me. You see, a long time ago, when Masud was just a child, his father had taken him to see a tomb in the Valley of the Queens. It had been shown to him by his father, who learned of it from a very good friend. It was an amazing sight, he told me. The tomb was full of things for the afterlife – a golden carriage, a boat, jewels, even food and urns filled with wine – treasures beyond imagination. Both Masud's father and his friend died suddenly after they had entered the tomb and Masud believed it had a curse on it.

When we were first married he told me about it one night but made me swear not to mention it to anyone, not even to our children if we were so blessed. He had decided not to do anything about it, just to let the dead sleep in peace. We have always had enough for our needs and don't believe that earthly possessions bring happiness. We have never spoken of it since that night. But now I think maybe someone else knew about it and that is why my husband and daughter have been abducted."

It took me some time to digest this latest piece of information. Unlikely though it may seem, it would help to explain their disappearance, especially since no ransom demand had been received. I asked Waleed if she had any idea where the tomb lies.

"No, my dear," she replied "only that it is in the Valley of the Queens."

I also asked her if she was sure that her husband had not mentioned it to either of their sons, but she was adamant that he would not.

"You know what young men are like, she said. "They would not be able to resist going to have a look and then they would want the treasures and the money it would bring them."

This seemed to make sense, as neither Pili nor Omar had mentioned it on our trip and had not shown any signs of looking for such a tomb.

"Do you have any idea where the family of your father-in-law's friend might be now?" I asked.

"Only that they lived not far from the Valley of the Queens," she replied. "I think the friend's name was.......um......let me think now. Yes, I'm almost sure it was Edjo. This was also the name of one of my cousins, which is why I remember it. But as for his family name, I'm sorry, I have no idea."

We talked more about what could have happened to Kareem, Masud and Yasmeen. It seemed we were just going around in circles.

"I beg you, my dear, use this information cautiously. In the wrong hands it will do a lot of harm and will not help our loved ones."

I rang John Turner and arranged to meet him for dinner. I didn't tell him over the phone the secret that Waleed had revealed to me and I wasn't sure if I would tell him later. What, if anything, was I going to do about it? I needed to get away and think so I left the house and wandered out into the streets of Cairo. There was a museum not far away with beautiful gardens and I made for this, ignoring the taxis calling out to me, so that I could sit under a shady tree and sort out my thoughts. I found a seat under a huge tree and closed my eyes. It would be foolhardy for me to try and do anything with this information on my own. But who could I trust? I thought of Kareem's aunt and uncle. They were likely to be of little help – they were quite elderly and I couldn't imagine what assistance they could offer. Hamadi? I hardly knew him and certainly didn't think I should trust him with this sort of information.

That only left John Turner. How well did I know him? He made you feel you could trust him – but could I? Working for the Australian Embassy he should be more interested in the welfare of two missing Australians than antiquities. Another possibility occurred to me – I could ring Jim and relate the story to him and seek his advice. It was not really something I could tell him over the phone though and I knew if I flew back to Sydney now I would find excuses – money, work, the impossibility of it all – not to return to Egypt. I felt I owed it to Kareem to try and find out what had happened to him and to his brother. If I did nothing and never found Kareem I would be forever haunted by guilt.

I battled with these thoughts for over an hour. In the end I came to the conclusion that the only person I could turn to was John Turner. I thought of his twinkling blue eyes and warm smile and I felt sure he was someone I could safely confide in.

I returned to the house and found Omar and Pili had finished in the shop. They seemed pleased to see me again and asked if I had made any progress.

"I'm afraid I haven't," I told them truthfully. "But I'm not finished yet."

We sat and talked for a while and I asked them about the missing dagger and collar.

"Are they very valuable?" I inquired.

"Yes, we believe so," said Pili. "They are certainly very old and the jewels are very fine specimens. We could understand if someone had kidnapped Yasmeen to obtain them, but if my father took them with him, why have they not both returned safely to us?"

I shook my head – I couldn't answer. I caught a taxi to the Marriott Hotel, where John had booked a table for us in the beautiful gardens overlooking the pool. He had chosen a table away from other guests where we could talk without being overheard. It brought back memories of my time there with Kareem and I found myself blinking away the tears.

Over dinner I told John all that I knew.

"I sensed there was something she wasn't telling me," he said. "It is not impossible of course – it is well known that there are many more tombs yet to be discovered and every few years a new one is uncovered. What Mr Ahmose and his father have done in keeping the whereabouts of this one a secret is highly commendable and not many would have done the same thing in their shoes. Whether his father's friend died without telling another living soul is something we cannot be sure about."

I toyed with my very rich chocolate and

fresh cream dessert.

"I just don't know what to do with this information," I said eventually, licking some of the ice-cream off the spoon.

John was quiet for a while. Then he reached across the table and took my hand in his.

"If you want to know what I really think......." he said.

"Go on," I encouraged him.

"Well," he said slowly "I think you should go home to Australia. Go back to your job and your friends and if anything comes up here I will let you know straight away. But" he went on carefully "I think you also have to accept that Kareem is probably dead and his brother also."

I gave an involuntary gasp. John had vocalised what I had been thinking subconsciously for some time. It seemed the logical answer but I wasn't ready to accept it. Surely Kareem couldn't be dead, not after we had just found each other.

"Many tourists disappear in Egypt every year," John continued. "The death rate from murders by cab drivers and locals for money and passports is quite high and many of them are never solved. The Australian Embassy does its best in these cases and has a higher success rate than many countries, but a large number are never resolved."

I pulled back my hand. I had to admit that John was a very attractive man and it seemed that he was quite interested in me, other than as an Australian citizen or even a friend. But I was not prepared to believe that Kareem was dead and the thought of being involved with anyone else had not crossed my mind.

"Thank you for a lovely dinner," I said as I made a move to leave. "It has been great to see you again and I really appreciate your interest in my problems. You are a very good friend. I will go back to Waleed's now and return to Luxor tomorrow and decide what to do next."

John, as always, was a perfect gentleman and insisted on walking me back to the Ahmose house. I knew as he left me he wanted to kiss me but I pulled back quickly before he could make his move.

"Thank you, John," I said quickly as I knocked on the door.

"Goodbye for now Anna," he replied. "Don't forget I'm here for you if you need anything." With that he turned and was gone and Waleed opened the door and I joined her for coffee before going to bed.

It was not the best night's sleep. I tossed and turned and had brief nightmares that woke me up but which I couldn't remember and I was relieved when it was finally time to rise.

Waleed pulled me to one side after breakfast and asked me what I was going to do next. I had to tell her that I really didn't know. I would go back to Luxor and think about what she had told me. I said that John Turner had suggested I go back to Australia and resume my life but that I was not sure I was ready to do that yet.

"You are strong," she told me. "I am sure you will make the right decisions. I just pray that our loved ones will soon be back with us safe and sound."

Omar, Pili and Waleed gave me a good send-off in the morning. I felt I knew them quite well by now and our shared grief and worry helped to bring us close.

When my taxi pulled up at the hotel Hamadi was there to greet me in the foyer. He was grinning from ear to ear and was bubbling over with his news.

"Mr Kareem", he said "Mr Kareem is back. He is waiting for you in your room."

I took the stairs two at a time, not wanting to wait for the slow lift, and opened the door. Sitting on the bed smiling at me was Kareem.

"Oh, my goodness!" I exclaimed when he released me from a huge bear hug. "Where on earth have you been? I've been so worried about you."

"It's okay now, he answered. "I'm back and everything is going to be alright."

From the way he kissed me I knew that he had really missed me.

"But where on earth have you been?" I asked when he finally let me draw breath.

"In a small hospital," Kareem replied. "I had amnesia and couldn't remember who I was."

"But John checked with the hospitals," I told him. "No-one answering your description had been admitted to any of the local hospitals."

"This was just a very small local hospice – basically run by two nurses and a doctor who came in once every few days."

"Well, how did you get there?" I wanted to know.

"When I took the ransom money to the temple I never saw Ramy, nor anyone I thought might be looking out for me. I stood near one of the tall columns at the back of the temple and then, suddenly, I was pushed from behind and the money was gone. I went headfirst into the dirt and it took me a few seconds to get myself together, but I ran after him. I saw my bag disappearing into a car and, as luck would have it, a taxi pulled up to let a man out. I jumped in and said "follow that car" – just as they do in all the American movies. Anyway, we went for quite a way and then the car turned into a small town. Anna, it was quite amazing. There was a small square and a big building with 'Camels and horses for hire'. Can you imagine – camels for hire!" Anyway, the man with my money got out here and went inside the building. I paid off the taxi and followed him. It was dark inside the building and it took a while for my eyes to adjust.

"This one for you, sir?" said a man who was holding on to a slightly underfed camel. "He very nice camel."

"No, no," I cried. "Where did the man go who came in before me?"

"Out the back, sir," came the reply.

I ran through to the back of the shop and out the back door into a dusty alleyway. Next thing I knew I woke up with the camel man staring down at me.

"Oh, thank goodness," he said "you have woken up. I thought you were dead – you have been unconscious for more than five minutes."

Well, I may have been awake but I didn't have a clue where I was or why I was there. When I asked the camel man what I was doing there he said he didn't know, I had just come running into his shop asking where the other man had gone to.

"I will call you a taxi sir," he said "to take you home. Where do you live?"

It was at that point that I realised I not only didn't know where I lived but I didn't know who I was. The camel man was very kind – he made me a cup of coffee and let me sit there for about an hour, hoping my memory would return. But, try as I may, I couldn't remember anything. In the end he suggested I see a doctor who lived nearby. The doctor asked me lots of questions, but I couldn't answer them. In the end, with much shaking of his head and "tut-tutting" he said he would take me to his hospice, where I could rest quietly for a few days. I asked him how long it would be before my memory returned.

"I hope it will be soon," he replied "but sometimes....you know, these things...well, we'll just have to wait and see."

Every day one of the nurses would come

and talk to me and ask me if I remembered anything. "Did you dream about anything?" they would ask me. The answer was always the same – nothing.

The days were very long, Anna. My head would ache from trying to remember who I was and where I came from. Did I have a wife? Children? The doctor was fairly sure I wasn't from Egypt – he thought I was American and apparently notified the American Embassy. Then one day a woman came into the hospital to visit one of the patients. She sat on his bed and took his hand and something in her expression turned a light on for me. She reminded me of you.

"Anna!" I cried out. "I need to find Anna."

The nurse came running to my bed and from then on little fragments kept coming back to me. Within a few hours my memory had completely returned. As soon as they could get in touch with the doctor to sign me out, I caught a taxi straight back to here. Only to find you were in Cairo, of course" he added. "Anyway, Hamadi was pleased to see me and so I spent the night here to await your return. And now, my love, what have you been up to?" he inquired, gazing intently into my eyes.

I quickly filled him in on the events of the past few days since he had gone missing, only leaving out Waleed's disclosure. I felt it better to tell him this later when he had fully recovered.

"Enough talk, now you must get some rest."

"Yes, nurse," he responded. "I was just thinking the same thing. Come to bed."

A couple of hours later we were drinking coffee in the café and pondering our next move.

"How long do you have to rest for?" I asked him.

"I'm fine," Kareem assured me. "Now that my memory has returned I just have to make sure I don't take any more blows to the head."

"Ha, ha, very funny" I replied.

I was ecstatic to have Kareem back. I kept glancing at him, to make sure he was really there! I decided he was rested enough now for me to tell him about the secret tomb. He listened intently.

"Wow!" was his comment when I had finished. "Now we could really be on to something."

"But what can we do with this information?" I asked him.

"We have to treat this carefully. No-one has been able to find out anything about Ramy, Yasmeen or Masud since they disappeared. Our only line of investigation is this tomb, but where do we start?"

Kareem was thoughtful for a while. The idea of a secret tomb full of treasures was a little hard to comprehend and I felt sure he was trying to figure out what could have happened to Ramy.

"If my brother is still alive," he said at last "then I must continue my search for him. Judging by the way they attacked me it would be easy to imagine that something has happened to Ramy too. If he is no longer alive, there seems little point in us putting our lives in jeopardy. However .... I cannot face my mother without being able to tell her definitely what has happened to Ramy. Therefore, I must keep looking for him. I just have to work out what to do next. But I think it is time you went home, back to work and the safety of Australia. I will follow you as soon as I find out something about Ramy."

I had been thinking of going back to Australia before Kareem reappeared. Now, however I couldn't bear to be parted from him again so soon.

"No, Kareem, I'm staying with you. We are in this together. I still have a little more leave. I want to stay and help you."

I could see Kareem, although worried for my safety, knew I had made up my mind and that, deep down, he was pleased I was going to be with him.

Section II Life Decisions – Ramy's Story

Yasmeen

It was a dream come true – to be in Egypt again, seeing the land of my forebears as an adult. I had been to Egypt once before, when I was very young, but this was so different! I spent a month with my uncle and aunt in Cairo exploring the city and soaking up the atmosphere.

It was hot - very hot - and there were tourists everywhere. The streets were noisy and filled with vehicles which followed no rules that I could understand – cars just crossed lanes when they felt like it, pushed their nose in front of the next car, did a u-turn in front of three rows of traffic – to me it was just chaos. Every time I went out on to the street taxi drivers called out to me – although I am tanned and have some of my ancestor's Egyptian looks, I guess my Australian shirts branded me as a tourist – at least from a distance. I thought I fitted in well in my jeans but apparently not. I visited the pyramids and marvelled at their grandeur. I went to the Museum and saw the Tutankhamen display, the mummies and the statues. I visited King Farouk's Palace and witnessed the wonderful displays of knives, guns and ceremonial gifts. My uncle was a great fan of the Egyptian hookah and I spent many hours sitting in cafes with him sharing this waterpipe, which I found very relaxing. After a month of enjoying all Cairo had to offer I decided it was time to go and see more of Egypt.

I bought a plane ticket to Abu Simbel and bade farewell to my uncle and aunt and headed off as an independent traveller. Abu Simbel was everything I had expected – and more. The sight of the huge statues rising out of the desert was truly amazing. To think they had been moved to their present site, piece by piece, from where they would have been flooded when the dam was built, defies belief. I looked closely and could just see where the cuts had been made; huge sections had been cut straight through, moved and then put back together.

Even now they are still very close to the water's edge – I tried to imagine the reactions of anyone travelling up the Nile, coming around the bend in the river and suddenly seeing these huge, imposing monuments in the middle of nowhere. The Great Temple has four colossal statues of Ramses II, seated. Between his legs are several much smaller statues representing his family. I wandered inside, along with the hordes of tourists, to marvel at the interior - two rows of pillars ten metres high with the features of Ramses. Above, on the ceiling, are great vultures and the aisles on either side are painted with stars. From there I entered the Sanctuary – a small room about four metres by seven metres in which sit statues of Ramses II, Ptah, Amon-Ra and Ra–Harakhti. The Sanctuary is built on a pre-determined axis and twice a year, corresponding to the equinoxes, the sun rises and lights the statues of Ramses, Amon-Ra and Ra-Harakhti. Somehow, Ptah, the god of darkness, is never lit. All this I had studied in Cairo before leaving, so that I might have an understanding of the sights I had set out to see in the context of my background. However, all the reading had not prepared me for the grandeur of Abu Simbel.

I went to see the Small Temple, just a little further around the river bank. The Temple was dedicated by Ramses II to his wife Nefertari and the six statues, all standing, gave the impression they were walking out of the wall to meet you. Inside the chamber carved with images of Nefertari as Hathor, are engravings depicting stories about Nefertari and Ramses. In the small sanctuary Ramses is shown honouring Hathor, who is set between two pillars and seems to stand out from the rock.

As I stood admiring this beautiful image I turned towards the entrance to see something even more beautiful. There in the doorway was the most gorgeous girl I had ever seen! She was obviously Egyptian, with long black hair, huge black eyelashes and olive skin. The sun caught her profile and her face was bathed in the most extraordinary golden light. It seemed as if there was nothing else in the world at that moment other than her as everything else around ceased to exist. Her lips, full and sensual, moved enticingly as she addressed a small group in front of her. I let my eyes fall to her body and noticed the way her simple black dress clung to her curves. I moved towards her to listen to her voice. She appeared to be a tour operator and was speaking in very clear English. Her voice was almost musical and she turned towards me as I approached. Huge, almost black, eyes met mine for a moment and I was locked in her gaze. Till that moment I had not believed in love at first sight but from that first glance I wanted to be with this woman more than I had ever wanted anything in my life. I felt a need and a desire that I had never known before.I wanted to possess her and protect her at the same time. Surely this was my destiny – my reason for being pulled back to Egypt!

I followed the tour group around for a while, from what I considered to be a discreet distance. I learned her name – Yasmeen. I was also learning more about Abu Simbel than I had intended! I followed the group back outside into the sunlight and as they clicked away with their cameras Yasmeen came towards me.

"So, you want to learn all about Abu Simbel and not pay the poor tour guide?" she questioned me in a mocking voice.

'It's not Abu Simbel I want to learn about,"

I replied "it's the tour guide herself."

She looked straight into my eyes and I felt the muscles in my stomach knot.

"You are more beautiful than Abu Simbel itself," I said. "I'm sure you have heard that line many times before but believe me, I really mean it."

There were no rings on her fingers so I took a deep breath and asked her to have dinner with me that night.

"Sure," she said "it's the only way I'll be compensated for the free tour."

She laughed a deep, throaty, sexy laugh and I found myself totally captivated.

We ate at a little restaurant Yasmeen knew where we wouldn't bump into any of her tour party. She was as exciting to be with as I had imagined. I learned that she was born in Egypt and her family lived in Cairo, having come originally from Luxor. She had been educated in Cairo and now lived in an apartment there which enabled her to take the tourist parties from Cairo to Abu Simbel. Sometimes the trips were just day trips, flying from Cairo to Abu Simbel and then back the same day. Mostly though, after Abu Simbel they flew back to Aswan and took a boat from there to Cairo via Luxor, visiting the Luxor and **Karnak** Temples and the Valley of the Kings before flying back to Cairo from Luxor. On this particular trip another guide was to take this group back and Yasmeen was to have the day off in Abu Simbel before picking up another group that night which was taking a boat back to Aswan.

The evening went well and Yasmeen seemed interested in me too. I told her of my life story to date – it didn't take very long. All too soon the meal was over and I walked her back to her accommodation. She let me kiss her and it was like no other kiss I had ever experienced. I hoped it was the same for her. I asked if she had plans for her day off and she replied softly "Yes, I have a very special one-on-one tour in mind,"

I picked her up at ten and we made our way down to the River. Yasmeen had a basket with her and I could see it was packed with food. She knew someone who had a felucca and he sailed us a little way down the Nile. The breeze was gentle and it felt as if we were just floating along. After about an hour our guide pulled up to a big flat rock and we clambered onto it. There was a small tree to give us some shade and with a wave our guide left us to our picnic.

"Pick us up in about two hours,' Yasmeen called out to him.

We smiled at each other like two children who had just wagged school! Yasmeen pulled a tablecloth from her basket and a bottle of wine from a coola bag. I pulled the cork and we sipped our drinks with the water lapping gently around us. Our own oasis! For a moment I was tempted to have a dip in the water, but then I remembered the warnings about swimming in the Nile. It is said that although the local children often swim in the water for those not brought up swimming in the Nile it can result in some very nasty illnesses, even death. It was probably cleaner this far up but I decided not to take the chance. Besides I hadn't brought my swimmers! We talked as we ate; it was so easy being with Yasmeen. She flirted gently with me as she told me stories of her family and her plans for the future. She did not want to be a tour guide for the rest of her life. Her family owned an antique shop and Yasmeen had soaked up antiques and artefacts all her life. She longed to be working in the shop but her father and two brothers were running it and it could not support her as well. She believed she had a gift, she told me, of picking rare and valuable objects, which her father encouraged but he did not understand her passion or flair.

"It sounds a bit big-headed, doesn't it?" she asked me, staring up at me from under her long eyelashes.

"Not at all," I replied, as I reached for her and pulled her closer to me.

I kissed her soft lips and she responded. After a few minutes we pulled apart.

"We had better eat some of this feast, I think, Yasmeen, before I get too carried away."

We finished our meal in silence, drank down the last of the wine and sunned ourselves on the big flat rock, watching the water sparkling in the sunlight. It was a perfect picnic, but all too soon our felucca was back to pick us up.

As we sailed back up the river I watched Yasmeen as she sat with her eyes closed against the sun, enjoying the breeze. 'She is so beautiful' I thought. 'She is the woman I want to spend the rest of my life with – and I have only known her for a few hours.' When I asked her to come back to my hotel she looked straight into my eyes for a moment, then dropped her gaze and took my hand. Together we walked back to the hotel. When I took her in my arms it was as if we were made for each other, our bodies belonged together and we spent the rest of the day in a blur of passion and intimacy.

The evening came all too soon and I walked Yasmeen to her boat where she was to pick up her next tour group. The thought of being separated from her so soon was more than I could bear so I had determined to catch a boat down to Aswan to be with her overnight. I couldn't get a berth on the same boat but I was lucky enough to get one on a boat leaving an hour later. Yasmeen had been able to book me on to her boat from Aswan to Luxor. The trip to Aswan seemed to take forever as we were always trailing Yasmeen's boat – at the temple stops I could see her boat pulling out as we pulled in.

The trip itself was interesting, even if the time inbetween sightseeing dragged a bit. The Kasr Ibrim, and the temples at Amada dedicated to Amun-Re and Re-Harrakte were well worth seeing. I learned that the Roman Temple of Kalabsha was originally built in Nubia and, although it was never finished, it was moved some fifty kilometres in 1970 when the Aswan Dam was built. It now stands one kilometre south of the High Dam, with a chapel and gate from it having been relocated to Elephantine Island. These things I would never have seen if I had kept to my original intention of flying directly back to Luxor.

After three nights we arrived in Aswan. We were taken in horse-drawn carriages for a tour of the city. I was appalled at the condition of most of the horses – so thin I wondered how they could do their work. I was tempted to refuse the trip but then I thought that the more money the drivers made the more chance there was of their horse being fed. There were shops all along where the boats tied up so there was lots of colour and activity. Unfortunately it was impossible to shop because the stallholders wouldn't leave you in peace to browse and were calling out to you as soon as you drew near. The dam itself was huge and quite amazing to see. We went across it in a bus and could see it was closely guarded. We pulled up in a purpose-built carpark and were able to walk and peer over the top on the huge body of water below.

Eventually I joined Yasmeen on the boat

on the other side of the dam as she was seeing her group into their cabins. She winked at me as I squeezed past her to go to my own cabin and my heart raced. That afternoon they were booked to go on feluccas around the Botanical Gardens and I joined Yasmeen on hers. It was a beautiful sight – the white sails of the feluccas fluttering between the bright blue sky and the blue of the water. I was so pleased to be reunited with Yasmeen and I felt sure by the glances she gave me that she felt the same way too. That night I crept into her cabin and by the way she came to me I was sure of it.

The next few days were some of the best in my life. The days were filled with sightseeing and the nights with passion and love. The warm, balmy evenings spent on the deck of the boat were relaxing and peaceful. Yasmeen treated me the same as any of her tour group, managing to spend a few minutes with me here and there as she circulated amongst them. I am sure many in the group had cottoned on to our relationship by the looks we exchanged but she was very professional and never allowed her feelings towards me to show during the days – although it was very different
through the nights.

The first day we took a motorboat to the Temple of Philae, dedicated to the Goddess Isis, which was relocated in 1960 and landscaped so that it appears similar to the time when it was built. Later in the day we visited the temple of Kom Ombo, which is really two temples, one dedicated to Horus (the falcon-headed god) and one to Sobek (the crocodile-headed god). Dinner on board that night was an Egyptian style dinner and Galabea Party and most of the guests dressed up in Egyptian-style clothes they had bought at the onboard shop. Yasmeen was resplendent in a white dress, with a gold sash whilst I spent most of the night holding on to my improvised outfit fashioned from one of my sheets. I wasn't the only one to be wearing a sheet but I seemed to be having more trouble than most in keeping it together! Eventually Yasmeen came to my rescue, tying her own sash around my middle. This freed up my hands for some dancing and I managed three dances with Yasmeen before she was whisked away by other guests.

The next day we visited Edfu and marvelled at the two black granite falcons guarding the entrance of the Temple of Horus, the Falcon God. Yasmeen was a knowledgeable and interesting guide, giving her group just enough information to whet their appetite without boring them. I pitied some of the tour groups around us – standing in the hot sun whilst their guides tried to impress them with their knowledge of Egyptian hieroglyphics and history. I was sure that most people who wanted in-depth information would either have read up on it before they left or would do so on their return. For the rest of us, a summarised version of what we had come to see was more than enough! Just being there, soaking up the atmosphere and seeing these sights with their own eyes was why people flocked to Egypt.

On our last day we were driven to the Colossi of Memnon, two giant statues in the middle of nowhere. From here we went to see the mortuary temple of Queen Hatshepsut. Once again I was amazed at the size of the Temple, situated in the middle of the desert. How the Egyptians – my forbears – had managed to carve these amazing temples miles from anywhere in the unbearable heat was beyond my comprehension. From a distance the temple was very impressive, set into the rocks and being of a considerable size. I was disappointed therefore that there was actually very little to see once you arrived at the building, apart from the three levels of terraces. One of the chapels could be seen by looking through the gate but it was not possible to walk inside.

However, the best was yet to come as we proceeded to the Valley of the Kings. In a valley of rock lay the tombs of the Kings, in splendid isolation and peace. To look at the Valley as we drove down into it you could not imagine there was anything of any significance amongst all these hills of rock, where nothing grew – not even the odd bush. However, as we drew closer we could make out tiny openings in amongst the rocks and as we followed the road down into the Valley we could see man's thumbprint on the landscape. A modern entrance marked the beginning of the tourist area, where we bought tickets to view some of the tombs. The entrances to the open tombs were walled and clearly marked, in stark contrast to the rest of the wild hills.

We were able to see three of the tombs during our time in the Valley. In the first one we went down many rough stairs into a large chamber and then down further to the burial chamber. Along the walls were brightly coloured hieroglyphics, still fresh and easy to see after so many years. The second tomb was very similar but the third was the one that really impressed me. We climbed up steep steps to reach it, crossed a cutting between two large hills and then descended even more steeply into the half-light. Down and down we went on these roughly hewn steps. Beside them were the original steps used by those who made the tomb, mere imprints in the dirt. How they climbed them with heavy baskets full of broken pieces of rock I don't know.

Finally we came into a large chamber where every wall was filled with hieroglyphics. From there we descended yet again, the low roof giving the feeling of the tunnel closing in on you. The chambers at the bottom though were worth the effort. Two small chambers led into a much larger chamber in which lay the empty sarcophagus. Again, all the walls were covered in hieroglyphics. A further smaller chamber at the back still housed a 'God box.' I was suddenly aware of Yasmeen studying me, watching my expression as I took in this mystical place – a place she saw regularly and had probably come to take for granted. I could see that on this occasion she was seeing it through my eyes, as a tourist experiencing it for the first time.

As we ascended back into the brilliant sunshine I could only marvel at the work that had gone into making these tombs out of such inhospitable ground. I would love to have stayed to explore further, but our time was up and we all traipsed back to the bus for the return trip to Luxor and the Temple of Karnak. What a huge day! Karnak was also amazing. The Hypostle Hall, with its seventy-foot high columns, is the largest temple in the world. From Karnak, Yasmeen was taking her group by plane back to Cairo to stay overnight and then finish their tour with a day's sightseeing of the Pyramids and Sphinx. I flew back with the group and spent the night at Yasmeen's apartment in Cairo. Whilst she was going around the Pyramids the next day, which I had already seen during my month in Cairo, I tried to sort out my feelings and my intentions. 'Is it possible I could really love this woman, whom I have only just met?' The answer was an emphatic 'Yes'. I had never felt this way before and was sure I wanted to spend the rest of my life with her. 'So what now?' I asked myself. I realised the first thing I have to do is to find out if Yasmeen was as serious about our relationship as me. Then we have to decide where we are going to live, Egypt or Australia. Was I really ready to leave my lifestyle and family in Australia to start a new life in Egypt? Would I, speaking no Egyptian, be able to find an accounting job in Cairo? Are there any jobs with English speaking companies? Conversely, would Yasmeen consider leaving her job, family and country to live in Australia? Well, I figured her job was not such a problem as it was not really what she wanted to do. Her family? They were close, but lots of women leave their country when they marry. I realised there was only one way to find out.

I went out in search of a good bottle of wine and some food with which I could make us a simple meal commensurate with my cooking skills and resolved that tonight I would bring up the matter of our future.

It was late when Yasmeen returned and I could see she was tired. She was pleased not to have to cook and the bottle of wine was better than I expected. After we had washed the dishes I asked her to sit down.

"Yasmeen," I began "I think you know how I feel about you – how much I love you. I cannot imagine a future without you in it. I really need to know if you feel the same way about me."

Without hesitating, Yasmeen replied:

"Yes, Ramy, it is the same for me. I love you too and I want to spend the rest of my life with you."

I was so relieved and excited I drew her into my arms and kissed her fervently. When we pulled apart I asked her where she thought our future lay.

"My future is with you Ramy," she answered. "I am happy to live with you in Australia if that is what you want."

By way of reply, I picked her up and carried her to her bed. My future was now decided!

The Disagreement

Yasmeen had wanted me to meet her family whilst we were in Cairo but unfortunately her parents had gone to the Bay of Dahab on the Red Sea for a week's holiday, leaving the antique shop in the capable hands of her brothers. We decided to leave this meeting until I could meet the whole family together.

The Valley of the Kings had captured my imagination and I wanted to explore more tombs and to walk amongst the hills where everyone knows there are still many undiscovered tombs. Yasmeen had a couple of days leave owing to her and we arranged to fly back up to Luxor on the week-end and stay overnight so we could have two full days exploring the area. We flew up Friday afternoon and booked into a hotel in Luxor, ready to set off for the Valley of the Kings the next morning. However the night before we left Cairo Yasmeen had received a phone call from a man in Luxor who said he dealt in special antiques and that he had something that would interest her father but that he had been unable to contact him. Yasmeen explained that he was away for a few days but that she was coming to Luxor the next day and would be happy to have a look at it. She had arranged to go to his stall at the markets the next morning.

"You go up to the Valley," she said "and I'll join you after I have been to the markets."

"I don't like you wandering around the markets on your own, I'll come with you and then we'll go on to the Valley."

"I prefer to conduct business on my own," she countered "besides I often go to the markets alone – don't forget I take tour groups there, I am well-known."

My macho-side kicked in then – this was the woman I loved and wanted to protect. I certainly didn't want her pushing me aside for a couple of hours. Before I knew it we were having our first argument.

'This is stupid," I finally realised. I needed to go out and get some air and calm down. I brushed past Yasmeen and went out into the night air. I walked around Luxor for a while and cooled off, getting things back into perspective. When I went back Yasmeen flew into my arms and I apologised for being such a chauvinistic male. Of course she could go and conduct her business and I would see her later. She had lived and worked in Egypt all her life – she knew better than me how to take care of herself.

However the next day Yasmeen had relented.

Okay," she said, "We'll go to the markets together and you can wander around whilst I go and meet with this Abdul."

We headed off and soon we were amongst the bustle and thrust of the hawkers. Most tried very hard to pull you into their stall, with promises of very cheap deals – grabbing you as you walked past and following you to the next trader offering better and better deals. There were many souvenirs of Egypt – wooden camels, statues of pyramids and of the Sphinx. There were also several jewellery stalls offering gold jewellery 'at the best price in Egypt.' Many of the stalls sold Egyptian cotton T-shirts and there were leather goods in abundance. I would have liked to look at some of the items but the stall holders made it impossible. They were in your face, offering you anything your eyes happened to fall upon at a cheaper and cheaper price, so you didn't have a chance to look around. In Yasmeen they recognised a fellow Egyptian and she stared straight ahead to where she was going, not looking to the left nor the right and they left her alone. In me, they obviously recognised an easy target.

Yasmeen was slowly getting ahead of me as I tried to fend off the traders. When she found Abdul's stall she turned and smiled at me and I was left to the mercy of the other stall holders. After fifteen minutes of their haggling I decided to wait at the front of Abdul's stall in the hope they would leave me alone. I looked inside for Yasmeen but couldn't see her. The stall was only small and I had been watching the front - I knew she hadn't come out yet. I went further in – there was a curtain and I tweaked the edge to peer behind it. There was no further merchandise there – it just led out to another lane. Obviously Abdul had taken Yasmeen to another place to show her his antique. I had an uneasy feeling – all the guide books warn you about going off with one of these stall holders to see other merchandise. It is a common ploy to take you out of view and rob you. Yasmeen of course would know this – but she would also have understood that a valuable antique would not be readily on display.

I walked through the curtain and out into the other lane. There were fewer traders here. I called out her name, as well as Abdul's but there was no response. I made my way up the lane. Then I heard what seemed to be a muffled scream. It was Yasmeen, I was sure. I bounded forward and around the corner – just in time to see her being manhandled by two men in Egyptian costumes.

"Yasmeen!" I cried, "Yasmeen!"

"Help me Ramy!" she screamed before one of the men slapped his hand over her mouth.

I found energy I didn't know I possessed as I ran towards her. They went around another corner and I tore around it blindly. There were no stalls down here and suddenly there was Yasmeen, still held by one of the men, looking at me with terrified eyes over his hand, which was still tightly over her mouth. Before I knew it a foot had been thrust out in front of me and I went down like a sack of potatoes. One of the men grabbed me and tied my hands behind my back with cord. I could see they had done the same to Yasmeen.

"What is going on?" I demanded to know when I got my breath back. "What do you want from us? If it is money, here, take it and let us go" I said.

They were dressed in traditional robes and had the mask used to keep the sand out of their nose and mouth pulled across their faces. All we could see were their eyes.

"We don't want you at all," said one of the men in reasonable English. "We want the girl, but you have seen us taking her and now you will have to come along as well."

They put gags in our mouths and pulled us around another corner where there was a car waiting. They opened the back doors and pushed us in, one of the men getting in with us and the other jumping in the front. A blindfold was put over my eyes but not before I saw the same being done to Yasmeen. Then we were speeding away from the markets, completely confused and very, very frightened. All the horror stories of tourists disappearing in Egypt flashed through my mind. Were they going to kill us?

When the car stopped we were pulled roughly out of the vehicle and pushed forward. The ground was uneven and I stumbled several times but the hand holding my arm yanked me upwards and stopped me falling. I could hear Yasmeen quietly sobbing. We were guided through a doorway and our blindfolds and gags removed.

"You can scream all you want," one of the men said "no-one can hear you now."

I looked around. We were in a small house, very rough and ready. They pushed us down on to two chairs in the middle of the room and tied us to them. Then they tied our feet. It was beginning to look very nasty. I could see Yasmeen was terrified but there was nothing I could do.

"What do you want from us?" I asked, trying to sound as if I was in charge.

The smaller of the two guys pointed at Yasmeen.

"You" he said "are going to tell us where your father got his latest antiques from."

"I don't know," Yasmeen replied. "I hardly every go to the shop now, I have a job as a tour guide."

This answer obviously didn't please him because he struck her on the face.

"Don't give me that," he countered "We know they are genuine and no-one has seen anything like them before. He must have found another tomb – one that has not been raided. We want to know where it is."

Yasmeen looked shocked and I felt sure she had no idea what the guy was talking about.

"I ….I don't know…" she stammered. "He has never said anything about it. I'm sure if he had discovered something he would have told me. He has never mentioned this to me," she stressed.

The man hit her again and I could see a large purple bruise already forming where he hit her the first time. I had never felt so helpless in my life. Not to be able to defend the woman I love was the most helpless feeling in the world.

"For goodness sake, Yasmeen," I hissed at her "tell him what he wants to know."

"I don't know anything," she replied, the tears welling in her eyes. "I can't tell them something I don't know."

"Very well," said the smaller of the two men. "Mosi, work on the boyfriend. Maybe when she sees you inflict pain on him she will be more co-operative."

Mosi crossed the floor towards me. He wasn't very tall but he was very stocky. Although his face was covered he obviously had a large nose because it protruded through the cloth. All I could see of his face were his eyes, which were brown, small and piggy. I could see the punch coming but there was nothing I could do to avoid it. It half lifted me off the floor, together with the chair, and I yelped in pain.

"Leave him alone!" cried Yasmeen. "I've already told you I can't tell you anything. Why didn't you ask my father, or my brother? Why are you asking me – you must know I don't work in the shop."

"Because you were much easier to grab," replied Mosi. "Your father and brother are in the middle of Cairo – someone would have seen us. But you move around in many areas so it was much easier to grab you."

"Very well, said the smaller of the men.

"We will take them to the cave and leave them there overnight. Maybe by morning she will have remembered something."

They undid our feet and untied us from the

chairs. Pushing us in front of them we went outside. It was easy to see why no-one would hear our screams. The little house was in the middle of nowhere. We walked for about an hour, Yasmeen stumbling occasionally on the rocky terrain. As we came to the top of a hill I could see where we were heading. Across the next valley on the next hill there were many caves. Again no-one would hear us scream and a feeling of dread descended on me. We were taken to the far end of the hilltop and up a steep track. The cave they had selected had a small opening and we were taken deep into the back of it then pushed into the blackness. As we fell to the ground there was a loud clang and a rudely improvised steel gate was locked on us, just inside the opening. From the outside it could hardly be seen and crude though it was I was quite sure I would never be able to force it back open. We were told to back up to the gate and, to our great relief, they untied our hands. We rubbed our sore wrists and I pulled Yasmeen into my arms.

As their footsteps faded into the distance Yasmeen and I looked at each other helplessly. They had left us a pitcher of water but no food. Things were not looking too good.

"Oh, Ramy," Yasmeen wept "what are we going to do? I honestly don't have a clue what they are talking about. I can't believe that if my father had found something he wouldn't have mentioned it to me. They must have the wrong family. How can we convince them?"

"We can't," I replied gloomily. "They'll be back in the morning to beat us again. We could die up here and no-one would know what became of us."

We lay down, wrapped in each other's arms. It had been a long day and night was starting to fall outside.

"We had better try and get some sleep. Maybe we will think of something in the morning" I suggested. Although we had not been given any food, fortunately neither of us was hungry, we were too stressed to feel like eating.

It was a long night for both of us. We eventually fell into an exhausted sleep, only to wake a short while after. I knew Yasmeen, like me, was remembering all that had befallen us – how our lives had changed since we set off so happily the day before with plans to explore the Valley of the Kings. The rest of the night passed restlessly as we drifted in and out of sleep, each time we woke the painful realisation of our situation enveloping us.

As light again returned to the outside world we were able to make out more of our surroundings. The back of the cave was very low and only about eight foot away. I went over to explore but could see only a wall of rock – no other opening. We had no option but to use the back of the cave as a toilet. Whilst we were petrified at the thought of our captors returning, we also knew we would be glad to see them for food and water and to know that we had not been abandoned.

It wasn't long after daylight that we heard footsteps and our captors returned. We could see they had water and some bread and cheese with them but they did not hand either to us.

"Back up to the gate so we can tie your hands again" instructed Mosi.

We did as we were told, hungry by now and hopeful of receiving the bread and cheese. Also our water had almost run out and we knew how thirsty we would be in the heat of the day.

Mosi unlocked the gate and came inside. The smaller of the men remained outside and closed the gate behind him.

"Now, lady, are you ready to tell us what we want to know or do we take up where we left off yesterday?"

"I can't help you," Yasmeen replied "I do not have this information."

Mosi hit her hard and she fell backwards to the ground. With his back to me it gave me the perfect opportunity to land a hard kick between his legs. Rather than fell him though, the blow had the effect of turning him into a raging monster and he knocked me to the floor and started kicking me.

"Stop it," cried Yasmeen. "He can't help you, he knows nothing – he doesn't even know my family."

When his anger had subsided Mosi withdrew behind the gate.

"Rashidi," he addressed the smaller man "what are we going to do with these two now?"

Rashidi seemed to be the one in charge. Much taller than Mosi, his eyes – more black than brown – were very unfriendly.

"Leave them to think about it," was his response.

With that the men disappeared back down the hill, leaving us sore and bruised and with our hands tied behind our back. With no water or food we were in a sad and sorry state.

"We need a plan," I said to Yasmeen after a couple of hours. "We can do nothing whilst we are locked up here. We need to find a way out."

We sat in silence for a while and then the beginnings of an idea started to form.

"What if we said we would take them to this tomb?" I asked.

"At least that would get us out of here," Yasmeen replied. "Maybe someone would see us and we can get help."

"Where can we say it is?"

"Well," she said, thinking out loud "it would have to be somewhere not too isolated, somewhere I am familiar with so that if we can break free we can find our way out."

"Well then, it would have to be either the Valley of the Kings or the Valley of the Queens," I suggested. "How well do you know your way around the Valley of the Queens?"

Yasmeen thought for a moment.

"Not as well as I do the Valley of the Kings, because most of our tours go there. But of course, we usually go to the same three tombs although I have occasionally explored further. The Western Valley tombs are the ones less often visited. Perhaps if we suggest it is in this area they are more likely to believe us. But we need to plan this carefully or we could end up buried in the Valley if they realise we are just leading them on."

She turned to me in tears.

"Our families would never know what happened to us."

"They won't know if we are killed in this cave, either," I pointed out. "At least if we can get out of this cave we have half a chance."

"What are you doing?" Yasmeen asked.

"I'm looking for a sharp piece of rock or shale. Ah, here is one – see how sharp it is on the end? I'm going to put it in my pocket. We can use it to try and cut through our ropes when the time comes."

I was quite proud of my forward thinking – it was certainly better than thinking about my family and how they would feel if I totally disappeared. In fact, they were probably already a bit worried about me. Since I had met Yasmeen I had been a bit slack in sending postcards or even ringing my aunt and uncle. I had been so wrapt up in Yasmeen I hadn't thought of anything else. Still, I guess that was a bonus because the sooner they started worrying about me the better!

"When will your parents start worrying about you, Yasmeen?"

"Soon. They are due back from their holiday tomorrow. Omar and Pili have probably been in touch with them but it is not unusual for me not to speak to them for a week."

"Do you think our captors will contact them direct?"

"I don't know what they are likely to do. They are not very educated. There must be someone else involved who can move the antiques if they get hold of them. They are obviously just the muscle – the ones who were told to follow me and grab me and then find out where the tomb is." Yasmeen reasoned. "They said they thought grabbing my father or brothers would be much harder, but by now they must be starting to believe me when I say I know nothing about this. Maybe they will try and blackmail them – offering me for the information on the tomb. I don't know."

This seemed to me to be a reasonable line of thought. Maybe we should just wait and see what happens before we try to escape. Perhaps it was not the right time to pretend we know where the tomb is – it might be better to hold this card up our sleeve for the time being.

I told Yasmeen of my thoughts and we agreed to keep our plan as a last resort. We would see what the men did next, maybe even suggest to them they should try and get the information from Yasmeen's father in exchange for our release. At all times the men had kept their faces covered from us so we would not be able to recognise them. At least that should give us a chance of being released alive.

It seemed an age before the men returned but it was probably only a couple of hours. By then we were very hot and thirsty, not to mention hungry. Mosi unlocked the gate and pushed through a pitcher of water before locking it again.

"Turn around and I'll take off your ropes," he said.

As he untied them he said, "There will be no food until you are ready to talk" and with that both men disappeared.

They did not return until the following morning. By this time all our water had gone and we were ravenous.

"Are you ready to talk now?" asked Rashidi.

"Believe me," I replied "if we had anything at all to tell you we would do so now. We are hungry, thirsty, dirty and tired. We need a bath and clean clothes. Why would we keep anything from you?"

He turned to Yasmeen. "You must know where your father got the golden collar and jewelled dagger from. Tell me where this secret tomb is and we will let you go right now."

Yasmeen was in tears. "I have no idea — those antiques have been sitting in the shop since I was a little girl. Please believe me, I can tell you nothing about them."

The two men stormed off, leaving us only a small pitcher of water. We were so dismayed we clung together, crying inwardly, seeking some comfort from each other, some respite from this dreadful nightmare.

The Secret Tomb

Later that day they returned. Again our wrists were bound. Then the gate was opened and Mosi grabbed Yasmeen and pulled her out of the cave, shutting it quickly behind her, leaving me on the inside.

"Where are you taking her?" I demanded.

There was no answer. Yasmeen was pushed along the path, almost too weak to walk. Alone and angry, I was beside myself with worry and grief. What were they doing to her? Where had they taken her? Would I ever see her again?

It was nearly dark when I heard footsteps returning. I craned my neck to try and see if Yasmeen was coming back to me. To my great relief and joy, she was. The gate was opened and she was pushed in. Her face was streaked with tears but there were no more bruises. Mosi handed us some bread and cheese, more water and another pitcher of water with a bowl and some rags.

"To wash yourselves," he said.

They untied our hands and left us. Yasmeen fell into my arms, weeping loudly.

"Are you alright?" I asked her gently. "Did they hurt you?"

"No," she replied "I am okay. I was just so afraid. I didn't know what they were going to do to me."

She had been taken to a house near the bottom of the hill, where there was a phone. Rashidi had told her he was going to ring her father's shop and tell him he would swap her life for information on the hidden tomb. After he had told her father he handed the phone to Yasmeen.

"Tell him you are okay," he said.

"I'm okay, Dad, but please, please do as they say. I am so frightened."

She could hear the emotion in her father's voice.

"Don't worry, I will do everything in my power to make sure you are safe and soon back home with us," he had assured her.

They agreed to meet early the next morning at the far end of the Valley of the Queens. Yasmeen's father would drive overnight to be there and Rashidi agreed to have Yasmeen and "her little friend" with him. Once they knew where the secret tomb was located, we would be allowed to return with Yasmeen's father. He was to tell no-one – if there was anyone else around or any police then Rashidi assured him that we would not live. He was also to bring with him the golden collar and the jewelled dagger.

We tore into the bread and cheese. We were ravenous and very low on strength. The food restored our spirits a little, especially now we had hope that tomorrow we would be free.

It was also great to be able to wash. As I watched Yasmeen undress and bathe herself I realised once again just how beautiful she was.

"Now that I'm clean I feel human again," she said, rubbing up against me. "Make love to me Ramy," she whispered, running her hands over my naked body. What was a man to do?

We fell into a deep sleep but were awake as soon as the sun began to lighten the cave. We had tried to save some food for the morning but we were so hungry we had eaten it all. We could only hope that our captors would be in a benevolent mood and bring us some breakfast.

Soon we heard footsteps and, to our relief, we saw that they had indeed brought us some gruel and water.

"Eat this quickly," we were told "don't waste time, we have a long walk ahead of us."

It was great to walk out into the sunshine, even though our hands were bound again. This time they didn't bother to blindfold us, I guess because they figured we would travel faster that way and we wouldn't be coming back anyway. It didn't really matter, the hills all looked much the same to me and most of the time I was looking at the ground so I wouldn't stumble. We walked for about an hour and as we came over the last crest I could see the Valley of the Queens spread out below us. Far in the distance I could see the first of the tourist buses coming towards Queen Hatshepsut's temple which was below us to the right. It was so far away that they looked like toy buses and I knew it would be useless to try and attract their attention if something went wrong. Let's hope these are men of their word, I thought.

I could see a man waiting under the overhang of a rock. The sun was already beating down on us and I knew Yasmeen must be as thirsty as I was. Nothing really mattered though except the thought that we would soon be free.

"That's my father," Yasmeen whispered to me.

Yasmeen's father was not at all like her in appearance. He was short and tubby but when he saw his little girl his eyes lit up and I could see the resemblance in his broad smile.

"My darling daughter," he said "I hope they haven't hurt you."

"Never mind about all that," said Rashidi "Give me the collar and the dagger.

Yasmeen's father produced them from inside his jacket and they glittered in the sunlight. Rashidi turned them over and over in his hands, examining them.

"They are truly remarkable," he said "and now it is time for you to show us where the tomb is that contains all these treasures."

From beneath their robes both Rashidi and Mosi produced guns and waved them at us, signalling for Yasmeen's father to lead us to the tomb. He nodded to me briefly in acknowledgement as we turned back into the hills the way we had come.

"It is hard for me to find this," Yasmeen's father was explaining to Rashidi. "I have not been here since I was a boy. My father brought me just before he died. The man who showed my father the tomb died suddenly and not long after my father brought me here he also died suddenly. It is believed there is a curse on most of these tombs and that is what I also believe. That is why I have not come back here. I have only those two items you have heard about, which my father took out and which came to me on his death. In fact I had all but forgotten about the tomb. These antiquities have been in my shop for years. People comment on them and I say they are not for sale, they are just part of the shop."

"That's enough talk old man," said Mosi "just keep walking until you find this tomb."

We walked to a ravine by a huge boulder, which looked for all the world like it was about to topple and roll down the valley. "We are close now" said Yasmeen's father. We walked between the sides of the sharp ravine and beyond it the ground opened up again.

"Oh," said Yasmeen's father, sucking in his breath "oh dear, what has happened here?"

Before us was a pile of rocks and shale in a huge mound.

"It was not like this," he explained "we covered the entrance to the tomb with rocks and stones so that it was hidden, but it was not buried under all these rocks. Some heavy rains over the years must have caused a landslip. The tomb's entrance was way below ground level."

Rashidi cursed and Mosi said "Great, what do we do now?"

Rashidi kicked at the rubble and cursed some more.

"After all this," he said, "we are no closer.

What is Mohammed going to say?"

At least we had the name of the top man. Not that it would help us much as every second person in Egypt seemed to be called Mohammed. We didn't know any of their surnames and I was sure they would soon disappear once they had cleared out the treasures of the tomb. But it was nice to have confirmation of our thought that Rashidi and Mosi were not smart enough to be acting alone.

"This Mohammed," I asked. "Where is he? We have brought you to the tomb, now you should let us go."

"Let you go?" said Rashidi. 'How do we know there is any tomb here? The old man could have brought us on a wild goose-chase for all we know. Now you will have to dig."

"Dig?" I repeated incredulously. "Dig that huge pile of rocks? We have an old man, a woman and me. We don't even have any tools. How do you propose we are going to dig through that?"

"We will get tools," Rashidi answered "and you will all dig. You are not going anywhere until we see the treasures in the tomb. Now we know where the tomb is supposed to be we can drive to the road behind the hills and carry the tools across. Mosi, you stay here with them and I will go and arrange everything."

"You'd better bring some water and plenty of food. We are weak from not eating," I retorted.

We sat in the narrow ravine to avoid the direct blast of the sun. Mosi positioned himself between us and the Valley of the Queens, his gun ready at his side. I introduced myself to Yasmeen's father.

"Please call me Masud," he said. "I am pleased to meet you – my daughter told me all about you over the phone before we went away."

At this Yasmeen kissed her father's cheek.

"I am so sorry papa," she wept.

"Don't be, Yasmeen," he replied. "It is me who is sorry that you are in this awful mess."

"I never even knew about the tomb," she continued.

"No, my daughter. Not even your brothers know about this. I decided to let the secret die with me. It has already cost two lives. I am sure my father died when he removed just two pieces of treasure because of a curse put on the tomb. That is why I have never sold them. I hoped the curse would die with him."

"But you could have been rich if you had sold the treasures – even if you had turned it over to the authorities you would have received a very handsome share."

"I know," he replied. "In some ways I suppose I was silly. But I made a promise to my father to keep it secret. I have enough money for what we want, I do not need any more. It is so sad that all the tombs are raided, even though many of the treasures go to museums. Surely we should leave some for future generations to discover, or even to lay in peace as it was intended?"

"Are you sure this is where the tomb is?" Yasmeen whispered, so that Mosi couldn't hear what she was saying.

"Yes," he replied, also in a whisper "I thought about taking them to the wrong place but your life to me is worth more than any treasure. Although I was very young when my father brought me here he showed me how to line it up with the Queen Hatshepsut's tomb to bring me to this ravine and then it was sixty paces from the end of it. I hadn't thought about it being covered over though."

"Stop the whispering - or you," Mosi bellowed, pointing at Yasmee "will be very sorry."

"So how did your father find the tomb?" Yasmeen asked after a few minutes. "Did he discover it with the other man?"

"Oh no," Masud replied "the other man, my father's great friend Edjo, told my father he knew of it only as a rumour which had circulated in his family from the times of the burials of the Queens in the Valley. He believed one of his ancestors may have worked on the tomb. Many had gone looking for it but without success. Edjo also had searched for it in vain. Then one day he stumbled across the ravine and he said as he came through it the sun shone on a very bright stone in a hole in the ground. Curious he went over to look at it and found that the ground around it was falling away. He marked the spot and came back the next day with a shovel and a pick. He camped here for a couple of days and it wasn't long before he found an opening to a tunnel. Some of the ground must have been washed away, much as it has now been heaped back on top of it. It doesn't rain here very often, but when it does it roars down. He told of a long tunnel going down deep into the ground. It opened into a big chamber which was filled with treasures he had only dreamt about. Off this big chamber there were two smaller chambers. One held the sarcophagus and the other more treasures to help her on her journey to the next world. He said the pictures covering the walls were still very vivid and beautiful to behold. He marvelled at the gold carriage, ready but not assembled. There was everything the Princess could need for her journey to the after-life – jewellery, gold combs and hair adornments, urns and pitchers full of food, wine and water, knives, forks, dishes – the chambers were bursting with beautiful objects.

Not wanting to draw attention to his find by taking anything too large, Edjo had simply taken the jewelled dagger, which he slipped inside his robes. He covered the entrance to the tunnel before returning to his village to consider what to do next. He told my father and took him there to see it. This time they took away the golden collar. The next day Edjo took ill. On his deathbed he told my father he believed he had been cursed for disturbing the tomb. "Take the dagger and the collar" he begged my father "and promise me you will keep the secret."

A few months later my father took me to see the tomb. He said someone else should know about it. He told me to remember the location of the ravine. Then we paced out the distance from the end of the ravine to the opening of the tomb. He told me never to forget it – to keep it as my inheritance.

My father died the next week – hit by a truck crossing the road in Cairo. You can say this was just an unfortunate accident but I took it as a sign and I never returned to the tomb, nor did I mention its existence to anyone, except once to my wife Waleed. We agreed never to talk of it again, nor to tell our boys."

"Then how did these two clowns find out about it then?" I asked him.

"I don't know," Masud replied. "But there was a man in my shop a couple of months ago who showed a great interest in the collar. He asked me if I had anything similar and I showed him the dagger. He wanted to buy them and became quite agitated when I said they were not for sale. He eventually went away and I didn't think anything more of it."

"What did he look like?" I asked.

"He was a big man," Masud replied. "He seemed to fill the doorway. He was very Egyptian looking – dark eyes, dark hair, not very good looking. I'm sure I'd recognise him again."

"If he's anything like the others, you won't

get a look at his face. They have been very careful to keep themselves covered all the time," I pointed out.

At this point Mosi told us to get up.

"We are going to meet the truck now so you can bring back the tools you will need. Start walking."

It took us about twenty minutes to get to the track which served as a road in these parts. Not long after we saw the cloud of dust as Rashidi returned. He had brought cold meat, bread and more water. Yasmeen and I fell on the food and the others ate their share. Then we were ordered to pick up the shovels and picks and head back to the tomb site.

"Now," commanded Mosi "start digging."

It was very hot and hard work. Masud soon worked up a sweat and I wondered how long he would be able to continue. Yasmeen was struggling but went at the task with her usual vigour. I was the only one able to move the bigger rocks and after an hour or so it was starting to tell on me. I looked at what we had achieved – very little.

"One of you is going to have to give us a hand," I said. "Give the old man a break."

Rashidi pointed at Mosi and ordered him to take over Masud's shovel. Between us we managed to make some impression but it was obvious that it was going to take us several days to remove the mountain of rubble covering the tomb. I just prayed that Masud was accurate with his pinpointing of the entrance! We took it in turns to spell in the shade of the ravine and drink water. At all times Rashidi watched over us with his gun ready should any of us try to escape. I don't think any of us had the energy to try and run.

Just before nightfall we were ordered to pick up our tools and walk back to the truck. I gave Yasmeen my arm – she was barely able to walk. Her father stumbled a couple of times and I could see he too was close to collapse. We fell into the truck and were driven about ten miles down the track. The truck stopped at a cave which looked similar to the one we had been kept in before. We were told to get inside quickly. Once inside we realised this was a proper house set into the hill. It had very little furniture – a couple of mattresses and cushions on the floor and a rough table with a four chairs. Apart from this room, which contained a small kitchen there was a bathroom.

"Wash yourself in the other room," Rashidi ordered Yasmeen "and then make yourself useful in the kitchen. You will find some meat and vegetables in the fridge."

I knew Yasmeen was almost too tired to stand, let alone cook, but somehow she managed to fix us some food and we sat down to our first proper meal in days. Just as we finished another man arrived. Apparently he was going to be our guard overnight. Masud and I washed the dishes and we all fell asleep almost immediately, physically and mentally exhausted.

This routine was followed for the next couple of days as we gradually cleared away the rubble. I thought about trying to leave in the middle of the night and go for help, but I couldn't leave Yasmeen and I knew she wouldn't leave her father. It seemed a hopeless situation. By the end of the day we were almost too tired to think. But gradually we became quite fit and we were given plenty of food to sustain us. Thank goodness it was not the middle of summer. As it was we rested in the middle of the day, taking shade in the ravine whilst we ate our lunch. In the forty plus degree heat of summer none of us would have survived. I think our night guard, Gahiji, felt sorry for us because after the first day he was at the house before we arrived and had a meal prepared for us. He had much kinder eyes than the other two and was very small and thin. If I get the chance, he would be the one I would have the best chance of taking, I thought, even though he's probably very wiry.

Finally we made the breakthrough we had been hoping for - we found the entrance to the tomb. Mohi and Rashidi were ecstatic.

"Come," Rashidi said to Mosi "we will go and tell Mohammed. He will be very pleased and he will want to be here when we uncover the tomb's entrance."

We were bundled back out to the truck and taken back to the house. Soon Gahiji came to guard us whilst Rashidi and Mosi headed off to tell this Mohammed. At last we were going to meet the mastermind behind this plan. Mohammed obviously had the contacts to move the treasures and I couldn't wait to see if Masud would be able to identify him as the man who had come to his shop.

"I will know his voice," Masud whispered to me. "If he speaks, I will know him."

It was not long before Rashidi and Mosi were back with Mohammed. He too had his face well covered. He was even taller than Rashidi and as stocky as Mosi.

"So," he boomed "we have found the treasures. Let us go and see them."

Masud caught my eye and gave an almost imperceptible nod. So this was the man who had come to his shop!

We headed back to the tomb and I looked in dismay at the biggest of the rocks blocking the opening. How were we going to move it even with an extra man? Mohammed must have seen my expression.

"We will soon move it. In here I have some dynamite" he said, pointing to the bag he was carrying. "Don't worry – I know how to use it – I will not blow up the tomb."

He laughed aloud at this. Then he carefully set the dynamite and we all stood back in the ravine whilst he lit the fuse.

'Perhaps the bang will bring someone to see what is happening,' I thought. When it went off though, it was only a small bang and although it echoed around the small valley, ricocheting back off the ravine walls I doubted that anyone would have taken much notice even if they had heard it.

The dynamite did the job and Mohammed quickly disappeared down into the blackness. We could see the light of his torch going down very steeply and then nothing. I prayed that Rashidi or Mosi would follow him down. Now would be our chance to get away if we only had one of them to deal with. I tried to remember who had the keys to the truck this time. I was pretty sure it was Rashidi. I looked around for a suitable rock to hit our guard with whilst we made good our escape.

But it was not to be. Rashidi and Mosi stood like statues at the top of the tomb but did not make any effort to enter it. When Mohammed finally returned he was visibly shaken and excited by what he had found.

"You have no idea," he said to his partners in crime "what treasures there are down there. It will take us weeks to remove them. I believe it is the tomb of a Princess. She has everything with her that she could possibly want in the afterlife. Go Rashidi – take the torch and go and see for yourself."

Rashidi came back equally stunned by what he had seen and then it was Mosi's turn to descend into the blackness. He was babbling when he came up again.

"We are rich," he cried "richer than our wildest dreams. Our families will never have to work again. We will all live like Kings."

Mohammed descended once more into the tomb and returned with a dazzling ruby and emerald necklace.

"I must have a little souvenir," he said to Rashidi and Mosi.

"Next time you two will have a little something but right now we must seal the tomb. There is wood and some nails in the truck, as well as a big lock – take Ramy with you and get them. We will make a gate."

When the gate was finally in place and locked we were taken back to the truck and returned to the house. Mohammed, Rashidi and Mosi stood talking outside waiting for Gahiji to come back to guard us. They stood far enough away that it was hard to hear them, but their excited voices turned to angry ones and we knew they were arguing amongst themselves, no doubt as to what their next move would be. When Gahiji arrived they went their separate ways. Yasmeen and I looked at each other. Gahiji spoke very little English so we were able to talk quite freely, although usually by the time we had eaten we were too tired to talk. We would fall asleep in each other's arms, hoping that when we woke up we would find it had all been a terrible dream and our lives would return to normal.

Masud spoke first.

"It is all as I left it then. No-one has touched it in all these years."

"Now that they have what they want, what will become of us?" Yasmeen asked.

"They promised to let us go," I replied quickly. "But I think they will need us for quite a while yet, to bring out the treasures and carry them to the truck. It will be a long slow job and it will depend on where they are going to store them and how quickly they can move them. They may already have buyers for them. You can be sure they are not going to tell the authorities about their discovery – they want it all for themselves."

"I don't understand how they found out about it," Masud said. "I have told no-one about the tomb or its treasures."

"I have been thinking about that," I said slowly. "Edjo must have told someone in his family. I can't see any other explanation."

"Well, although I was only small when I went into the tomb, I am sure it is still a long way down, with many steps, and it will not be an easy task to empty the tomb."

"What if they don't let us go afterwards" Yasmeen persisted. "We should have a plan to get us out of here."

I didn't disagree. It had already occurred to me that they may not be intending to let us go. If we were killed and our bodies buried near the tomb – who would ever find us? There was a very convenient pile of rubble already loosened by us to reveal the tomb that would be easy to hide three bodies in.

"Our only chance would be to lock them in the tomb when they are all down there and run to the truck," I whispered. "We will just have to keep our eyes open for such an opportunity."

Gahiji pricked his ears when he heard our whispers.

"Be quiet" he yelled out. "You no talk good."

We left it at that.

Golden Treasures

Early the next morning Rashidi, Mosi and Mohammed were back to collect us. The truck had acquired a cover overnight – a high canvas affair similar to an army truck. They obviously planned to pack a lot of treasures into it. When Mohammed opened the gate to the tomb he signalled to us to go in. "Come and see what you are going to move for us" he said. He handed us each headgear with a torch in the middle of it. Whilst Rashidi and Mosi remained at the top we made our way down the roughly-hewn steps deep into the ground. Masud led the way, keen to see what he had first seen so many years before.

At the bottom of the tunnel there was a huge chamber. Yasmeen and I gasped in awe as we saw the treasures it held. The gold carriage which Masud had spoken of was as breathtaking as he had described. The chamber was filled to capacity with the most amazing objects. As we turned around our torches picked up more and more artefacts and the golden objects glistened in the beams of light.

We made our way into one of the two smaller chambers. This was also filled with treasures. The other smaller chamber, as Masud had told us, held the sarcophagus. It was very small – similar in size to that of Tutankhamun, the boy King. It too was surrounded by treasures.

"By the work that has gone into the tomb it

seemed they had known she was going to die young and had been busy preparing it for her. Although it could have been prepared for someone else and she died first," Mohammed explained. "No matter, it is going to make us very rich. Now it is time for you to make yourselves useful. Start with the largest chamber and make sure you don't damage anything."

I wasn't sure how Masud was going to manage this. The steps were very crudely cut and it was a steep climb back up the tunnel. Then it was long walk to the truck. We obviously needed either more people or some other way of getting the treasures to the truck. Apparently Mohammed had thought of this.

"You," he said, pointing to Masud "come with me, you will drive the donkey cart."

Obviously he didn't want anyone else knowing about the tomb! The donkey cart was of long, thin construction and would just fit through the gap in the ravine.

'Well,' I thought, 'that suits us because as long as we are needed we are safe,' although I still harboured strong doubts as to whether they would let us go once the job was done.

Some time later Masud and Mohammed returned with a mule and narrow cart. It was Masud's job to load the cart, drive the mule to the truck and unload on to the truck. Sometimes Mosi would help him. Mohammed would then drive the truck to wherever they were storing the treasures and unload them by himself. It was up to Yasmeen, myself and Mosi to bring the treasures out of the tomb.

We constantly marvelled at the objects we were moving. They dazzled in the sunlight when we brought them to the surface. Mohammed had provided bags in which to load the jewellery and smaller items. The larger items, such as the carriage pieces, urns and even a raft, Mosi and I had to manhandle up the steps. Yasmeen would be in raptures over some of the treasures.

"This piece alone," she said, holding up a golden necklace "would be worth more than one hundred thousand Egyptian pounds. Can you imagine what they are going to get for all of this?" she exclaimed, waving her hands at everything around us.

We spent many days just emptying the large chamber. Then we started on the smaller one which held the sarcophagus. These were mainly small items such as combs, jewellery and even a mummified dog and cat.

"What are you going to do about the sarcophagus?" Rashidi asked Mohammed.

"We will leave it here," he replied. "I do not want to draw attention by selling a mummy and, if there is a curse on the tomb, maybe it will be placated if we leave the sarcophagus intact."

I was very relieved to hear that – not so much in relation to the curse but more the fact that I very much doubted Mosi and I were up to the task of removing it – even if we used rollers and tried to drag it up the tunnel.

We only knew what day of the week it was because on Sunday we were given a rest day as our Christian Egyptian captives thought we would work better if we had a day of rest. Although it was nice not to have to break our backs in the sun it was a very long day with nothing to do – no TV, unable to go out and only Gahiji for company. Yasmeen and her father slept most of the afternoon whilst I tried to devise a way of getting us out of this mess. Our only chance was to get hold of the truck but our captors were very alert to our every move and very careful about not leaving the keys in it. I could see no way of getting us all out together. So far I had not been game to try and implement my plan to lock them in the tomb whilst we made our escape.

They were very careful to leave Rashidi outside the tomb at all times to watch over us. He helped to load the cart but apart from that his main duty was to keep an eye on us. "'Perhaps," I thought 'once they have what they want they will just let us go. Although we know their names, we have never seen their faces, as they keep them covered at all times and they could easily be using false names to protect themselves.'

The final chamber had larger objects and it took us a few days to empty it. But eventually everything had been removed. I had no idea where all the treasures had been moved to but I figured Mohammed had a big storage area somewhere and would sell the items gradually so as not to flood the market and draw too much attention. No doubt he had buyers lined up for items for private collections.

After we removed the final objects Rashidi ordered Mosi and I to cover the tomb entrance with rubble. We toiled in the heat to conceal the tomb without moving any more rocks than we needed. With the job almost complete, Rashidi went off to help unload the donkey cart leaving Mosi to guard us. He ordered Yasmeen and Masud to help me finish covering the entrance. As they came to join me I took the chance to stretch my aching limbs. Then I moved to the side to make more room for the others. I made my way almost behind Mosi and picked up a good sized boulder.

Suddenly, in the heat of the day, three shots rang out across the desert.

Section III Life Decisions - Mine

Valley of the Queens

Kareem and I spent the rest of the day planning our next move. Early the next morning Kareem went out and hired a car. We took water and some bread, cheese and fruit and set off for the Valley of the Queens. With some difficulty we located the track that served as a road to go up into the hills behind Queen Hatshepsut's tomb. Far away from the tourists there were tracks into a small village and it was there we stopped at the local bakery to ask if they knew the family of Edjo. Our request was met with a blank stare – they didn't understand English and if they understood the word "Edjo" they were not letting on. You couldn't always tell with the Egyptians whether they really didn't understand or were using the language barrier as an excuse not to help.

The village was very small. Kareem wandered around, asking the same questions at the local shop and also of a couple of very old men sitting on a bench in the square. They raised their wrinkled faces and squinted at us through half closed eyes. Then one of them shrugged his shoulders, raising his hands as if to say "who knows, who cares?" All his inquiries were met with the same blank look.

"Okay," he said "this is obviously not going to get us anywhere. We need to find the Imam for this area and ask him. If he hasn't heard of

Edjo he may be able to check their records."

The village wasn't big enough for its own Imam so we returned to Luxor to inquire there. We went to the main mosque and sought out the Imam. We were told he wasn't available now but to come back at two and he would speak with us. We were glad to have our lunch and to discuss how we would broach the subject. After some deliberating, we decided to tell him that Ramy and Yasmeen were missing and we believed that Edjo, a friend of Yasmeen's late grandfather, might be able to help us find them. Promptly at two o'clock we presented ourselves at the mosque and soon after the Imam appeared and greeted us.

"Welcome," he said in good English. "How can I help you?"

Kareem explained he was looking for his brother and girlfriend who had disappeared. The Imam made the appropriate sympathetic noises.

"We think the family of a close friend of the girl's late grandfather may be able to help us find them but we do not know where they live now" Kareem said. "We thought you may be able to help us – either from personal knowledge or from the Mosque's records."

"I will do what I can," the Imam replied. "Tell me what you know."

"Very little, I'm afraid," "Kareem replied. "The girl's father is Masud Ahmose and his father's friend was called Edjo and he came from a small village behind the Valley of the Queens. That is all we know."

"I will go through the records tonight and see if I can find anyone named Edjo around that age. I myself have only been her for ten years and am not aware of him, but I will do my best to help you. Come and see me again tomorrow morning at nine."

We returned to Luxor, fervently hoping the Imam would be able to give us a lead. Without this, we really had no idea how we could proceed.

The Imam arrived at ten after nine and again greeted us courteously.

"You will be pleased to know I have some good news for you," he said. "There was only one person named Edjo in the records for that area who would be the right age. His family name is Ahmad and they live in the village behind Queen Hatshepsut's tomb. As you know Edjo died some time ago but he had two sons, Rohmald and Gahiji. As far as I know, they still live there."

We thanked the Imam profusely and returned to our room to consider our next move. Edjo's sons lived in the village where we had asked about Edjo and it seemed odd that no-one had recognised the name and directed us to either Rohmald or Gahiji. Not being able to think of any explanation other than our bad pronunciation, we decided to head off back to the village and start again. As we were about to leave the hotel, Hamadi called out to us.

"Where are you two off to in such a hurry?"

Kareem and I exchanged glances. We were not sure how much to tell Hamadi.

"We are going to the village behind Queen Hatshepsut's tomb to find Rohmald and Gahiji Ahmad, who may know something of my brother's disappearance," Kareem replied.

"Wait a minute and I'll come with you, Hamadi replied. "It will be much easier for me to translate for you – most of the villagers don't speak any English you know."

I can't say I was sorry to have Hamadi along. It would certainly be a lot easier if we had someone who could speak the language and we had no reason to doubt Hamadi's friendship.

We started at the local store. This time Hamadi went in, closely followed by us. He greeted the owner and then spoke to him, asking if he knew where we could find Rohmald or Gahiji Ahmad. We could tell by the nodding of the shopkeeper's head that he knew of them and, by the gesticulating of his hands, how to find them. Hamadi thanked him and we returned to the car.

"Gahiji still lives here," he said. "At the top of the next hill there is a track to the left. About half a kilometre further on there is a track to the right and Gahiji lives about a kilometre down the track in a whitewashed house."

I felt quite excited as we turned off on to the first track. Maybe at last we were going to get somewhere. I didn't know what Kareem would ask Hamadi to say. Would he mention a secret tomb or unrivalled treasure? I wished fervently that we had been able to talk this over before we met with Gahiji.

The house was easy to spot – it was the only one down that track and quite isolated. It was also very simple – small and untidy looking with rubbish all around it. I wondered if anyone still lived there. Hamadi and Kareem marched up to the front door whilst I waited in the car. Kareem knocked loudly. At first it seemed no-one was at home, but there was a twitching of the curtains and Kareem caught the man's eye so reluctantly he came to the door. Hamadi explained that we were looking for Kareem's brother and showed him a photo of Ramy and Yasmeen. "Yasmeen's grandfather was a very good friend of your father" Hamadi explained. The man invited them in and Kareem waved to me to join them. The man introduced himself as Gahiji Ahmad. He spoke some broken English. Kareem asked him about his brother.

"Rohmald?" he said, sounding surprised. "He is in your country, Australia. He lives in Sydney."

Kareem asked him if he had seen Ramy or Yasmeen. He seemed uncomfortable and unwilling to look closely at the photo.

"No, no," he said, waving the photo away. "What do you want from me?"

Kareem took a deep breath and took the bull by the horns.

"Did your father ever mention a secret tomb to you?" he asked.

The man made out that he didn't understand the question. Hamadi, having recovered from his initial surprise at the question, repeated it in Egyptian.

"No, no," Gahiji said again, becoming quite agitated. He feigned a laugh. "No secret tomb," he said quite adamantly.

We stood silently, not knowing where to go next with the conversation.

"And now, "he continued "I must get back to work."

With that, he ushered us through the small doorway and back out into the heat.

We climbed back into the car and Kareem started the engine and we drove back to the village. We were hot and thirsty and decided to stop at the local café for coffee. Kareem and I were feeling very flat. Hamadi, of course, was full of questions.

"What secret tomb are you talking about?" he asked. "Where did you hear of such a thing? Why would Gahiji know anything about this? How long have you known about this? Why did you not tell me anything?"

Kareem and I looked at each other. With a shrug of his shoulders, Kareem answered Hamadi.

"We don't really know anything about it, Hamadi. We are just trying to find out why Ramy and Yasmeen have disappeared, as well as Yasmeen's father. It seems Yasmeen's grandfather had a very good friend called Edjo, who was Gahiji and Rohmald's father. Yasmeen's mother told Anna that there was some talk of a secret tomb many years ago. Maybe it is just that, just talk, we don't know."

Hamadi was quiet for a while, sipping his coffee. You could almost see the wheels inside his head going around.

"What do you think is in this tomb?" he asked when he had drained his cup.

"We don't know," Kareem lied. "We are just trying to find some connection, some reason for their disappearance."

"Well, this Gahiji, he know nothing," said Hamadi. "and his brother is in Australia so he is no help to you. What are you going to do now?"

"I don't know," Kareem replied wearily. "We just seem to be getting nowhere."

"Let us go back to the hotel," said Hamadi. "I will cook you a nice lunch and then we will put our heads together."

While Hamadi rustled up some food in the kitchen, Kareem and I went up to our room.

"Did you believe Gahiji?" I asked him.

"No way," he replied. "He was far too cagey and obviously just wanted to get rid of us. His brother probably is in Australia but I'm sure he knows more than he is letting on. What did you think?"

"I agree absolutely," I told him. "He is up to something. But how are we going to find out anything more?"

"I think we have to go back and look around the tracks from the village," Kareem replied. "Because it hardly ever rains here, tyre marks stay on the tracks for a long while. If there is a secret tomb, and Gahiji knows something about it, we can assume has been there and there must be tracks somewhere from his house or the village out into nowhere land. Maybe we will be lucky and find them."

We decided not to tell Hamadi any more at this stage. The less people knew about the possibility of a secret tomb the better. Over lunch he asked us again whether we thought a secret tomb could be the reason why they were missing.

"Not really," Kareem answered, with a shrug of his shoulders that implied it was only the wildest of guesses. "It sounds highly improbable and we have no leads to follow."

"I could ask some questions for you," Hamadi volunteered.

"We really don't think there is any truth in it" I countered "we were just trying to get a reaction from Gahiji."

We steered the conversation to talking generally about the hopelessness of our task and how we should think about going home.

As soon as we could excuse ourselves we told Hamadi that we were going to talk to the Travel Agent and headed back to the Valley of the Queens. We found the track to Gahiji's house quite easily but were reluctant to drive past it again. We would be very conspicuous. Instead we drove past the track and after about a kilometre we saw another track. It was obviously used quite a lot, judging by the tyre marks. We followed it for about ten kilometres when it ran into a small cluster of houses. There was only one road out of this little village so we retraced our steps and went further on along our original track. The next track went off to the left and didn't look as if it was used much, if at all. After a short while it ended, so again we retraced our steps. It was then another five kilometres or so before we found the next track. This one was very narrow and also looked as if it didn't go anywhere but the tyre and cart tracks were profuse and where they met a large area had been flattened out by footprints. This was more hopeful! The track was too narrow to drive along so we left the car and started to walk. We were not too far down it when it turned sharply to the left and the track dropped quite steeply between two large rocks. From the road you would never know that the track continued. The track swung around to the right at the bottom of the two rocks and then widened out into a large flat area. Here the ground had been greatly disturbed. There were many footprints and many cart and donkey tracks. Something had certainly been happening here – but what? A meeting place, some kind of religious gathering? Or could it be our secret tomb? We sat on a small rock and surveyed the scene, trying to make sense of what we were seeing. There were several small hills, some obviously caused by heavy rains pushing down the small rocks and sand. However, most of the activity seemed to focus around one particular mound and we walked over to have a closer look.

"What if this is the secret tomb?" Kareem speculated "and all the activity was caused by the removal of its contents?"

I nodded slowly, thinking about this possibility.

"But there is no sign of an entrance," I said after a few seconds. "What if it was covered up afterwards? If you had found a secret tomb and wanted it to stay secret, wouldn't you cover the entrance up again before you left?"

"Maybe there are still some treasures down there," Kareem suggested.

There was only one way to find out, but we had no tools to dig with and the searing afternoon heat did not make it a very attractive proposition. Reluctantly we decided to return to the hotel and give the matter further thought overnight.

Over dinner we agreed on our course of action – we would buy a couple of picks and a shovel and go back and see if we could find an entrance to a secret tomb beneath the rubble. Next morning we were up early and, taking plenty of water with us, we bought the picks and shovel and headed back to try to discover our secret tomb. Kareem was worried about leaving the car near the track.

"If there is a tomb and Gahiji or whoever is involved sees the car parked there they will immediately know someone is near the tomb."

Fortunately there was a big rock not far from the track and we parked behind it, hoping that this would provide sufficient cover.

It was not much fun carrying the water, picks and shovel back along the track. When we arrived we sat on a rock, drinking some of the water, trying to work out the best place to attack the rubble. We looked at the footprints again.

"There are some footprints that stand out amongst the others, Kareem" I said excitedly. "Look, there are prints from trainers amongst the Egyptian sandal imprints."

"You are right," he replied. "That would indicate my brother and the girl could have been here – or that the robbers had bought themselves some western footwear," he added gloomily.

"Think positive," I advised, trying to sound positive myself.

We decided to start work on the middle section of the rubble where all the footprints seemed to go and set to work. We did not know if the entrance – if indeed it existed – would be barely covered or almost totally buried.

We worked for a couple of hours, with Kareem doing the bulk of the work. Fortunately for us, the entrance had only been covered with a minimum of rubble and when Kareem put his pick through into the hole he let out an excited scream.

"It's here," he exclaimed "the secret tomb does exist!"

We worked frantically to clear a hole big enough to climb through. Fortunately at the last minute I had thought to buy two torches and we were able to clamber through the hole and light up a long tunnel with steep steps. I didn't much care for the darkness or the thought that we were going deep into the earth but I followed Kareem as he led the way deep into the tomb. When we came to the main chamber it was empty. We found two smaller chambers, also totally devoid of any treasures. Only the sarcophagus remained.

"This must have been the tomb of someone important," Kareem commented. "Look at all the drawings on the walls. They are absolutely amazing and the colours are still so vibrant."

Getting over my disappointment at not finding any treasures I turned my attention to the walls and Kareem was right – the real treasure was probably in the stories told in the pictures, not objects which are easily broken or stolen.

Having satisfied ourselves that there were no treasures left in the tomb we turned to retrace our steps to the outside world. At the bottom of the steps Kareem suddenly bent over to retrieve something.

"My brother's St Christopher!" he said in amazement. "Ramy has been here – he must have lost this, or left it here for someone to find. He always wears this. Finally, I feel I am close to my brother and at last I have some idea of where he has been all this time. This must be the right tomb."

As we started up the steps there was a loud bang and then a rumble. We looked up towards the light to see a shower or rocks bouncing towards us.

"Get back," said Kareem "we must take shelter in one of the smaller rooms."

We ran into the room with the sarcophagus. The rumbling kept coming and we could hear small rocks bouncing off the sides of the tomb and down the steps. After a few minutes, everything went quiet and Kareem ventured out into the large chamber. I crept out behind him and he shone the torch up the steps.

"Someone just dynamited the entrance!" Kareem exclaimed. "I think the entrance is totally blocked" he informed me. "I can't see any light coming through."

We ran up the steps, panting and gasping for breath and dodging small rocks and stones. When we got to the top we could see the entrance was well and truly blocked. We looked at each other in horror.

"I think Gahiji or someone involved in this has seen us or the car and come to make sure we don't tell anyone about the tomb or ask any more questions about the others. I think we have been deliberately buried alive." Kareem said despondently.

The horror must have shown on my face as Kareem put his arms on my shoulders.

"I'm sorry, I'm so sorry Anna. I wasn't thinking. I'm sure we'll find a way out or they will come and dig us out when they have decided what to do with us. Please, don't worry, we'll think of something."

By now I was sobbing hysterically. The thought of being buried alive was terrifying.

"You know they won't come back for us, I cried. "They have left us to die and no-one knows we are here. We are going to DIE in this tomb," I screamed.

He held me tightly as I cried – great racking sobs of fear and pent-up anxiety from the past few weeks and Kareem's disappearance. Up until now I had been strong, but being sealed in this tomb was just too much to bear. At last I cried my last tear and dabbed ineffectively at my tear-stained face and swollen eyes.

"I'm sorry," I said at last. "I'm just so scared."

"So am I," Kareem replied, "but I am sure we can figure a way out of this. Did we bring the water inside with us?"

"Yes, I put it just inside but the picks are still on the other side of those rocks."

"Even if we had the picks with us I suspect there are sufficient large rocks over the entrance to ensure we can never dig our way out" Kareem said. "I'll go and see if the water survived the blast. Go and sit down and we'll think about how we are going to get out of here."

"The water is safe," he called out from the top.

'That probably just prolongs our agony,' I thought to myself. We sat side by side on the bottom step, two forlorn figures trying to cope with thoughts of our mortality, at the same time wondering what fate could have befallen Ramy, Yasmeen and Masud.

"I think my brother must be dead," Kareem said eventually.

I couldn't dispute it. If they were willing to kill us, why would they not have already killed the others?

"We don't know that," I said, a little unconvincingly. "We should try and work out what we think happened."

"First, we must have a good look around whilst we still have light from the torch," Kareem stated taking charge.

"Well, the batteries should last a while," I said "seeing as how we just bought them."

"The trouble with things in Egypt," Kareem replied "is that you don't know how long they have been sitting on the shelf."

I smiled weakly at his logic. It would have been better if he had just agreed with me.

"Okay," I said "let's go exploring."

We went up the steps again, stepping carefully over stones and rocks on the way. At the top the light was completely blocked.

"This looks hopeless," Kareem said. "We'll go and have a good look at the back of the tomb. If it is completely sealed we will have to start tearing these rocks away with our hands, in the hope that we can make a hole small enough for you to crawl out of and go and get help."

We trudged back down the steps and Kareem carefully examined the walls of the main chamber.

"I can't see anything here that would suggest another tunnel."

We moved on to the small chamber with the sarcophagus. Again Kareem could find nothing that suggested another opening in the walls. We went into the other small chamber, with the same result. Despondent we returned to our seat on the step.

"There is probably enough air down here that we can live quite a while," I said after a while, "and you are supposed to be able to go without food for a few days, although my stomach already thinks it's hungry."

"Mine too," Kareem agreed.

"It seems our only option at the moment is to try and move some of the rock," he said after a few minutes.

We climbed the steps to the top once again. We put the torch on a step to give us light.

"We need to try to keep the rocks we move to one side so we have access to the steps," Kareem decided. "Try and place them rather than throwing them."

We set to and started moving some of the smaller rocks. It was very hard on our hands and soon my nails were broken and my fingers were bleeding. Worst of all, the exertion made us thirsty. After a couple of hours we were tired, thirsty and hungry. We decided to try and ration the water and only took a couple of mouthfuls each.

"Let's turn out the light and try and get some sleep," Kareem suggested. "It will be cooler in a few hours and it would be better to work then."

We lent against each other and, despite our uncomfortable circumstances, soon fell into an exhausted sleep.

I woke first and sat blinking in the darkness trying to remember where I was. Even though I had drunk nothing for the last few hours I needed to go to the toilet. I eased myself away from Kareem and gingerly went down a couple of steps. There was no chance he could see me. I heard Kareem moving about.

"Anna, where are you?" he called out.

"I'm just over here – back in a minute," I said. I returned to snuggle up against him.

"Ah, I know what you were up to," he said. "I'll be back in a minute too."

There were no little alcoves in the tomb's corridor or its chambers - nowhere we could use as our toilet. It was going to become quite unpleasant in here pretty quickly. 'Not that we'll last that long anyway once the water is gone,' I thought to myself grimly.

We went back to work moving the smaller rocks. Soon there were only bigger rocks and we had no tools.

"Find a suitable rock to use as a wedge," Kareem instructed me.

We both found a discarded rock to use as a tool and Kareem managed to remove a couple of the larger rocks, but behind them there was always another solid wall of rock.

"This is hopeless," I said after a while. "I can't stand looking at this anymore. Let's go down into the chamber and have a break."

We picked our way carefully down the steps and went into the small chamber without the sarcophagus – it was less depressing. Sitting against each other we turned off the torch to conserve the battery. The thought of being totally without light was one that haunted me, probably even more than being without water.

"So what do we think happened to Ramy and the others?" I asked in the darkness.

"Well," Kareem replied "we know Ramy was here. I think they used Yasmeen to blackmail her father into telling them where the tomb was."

"Perhaps they used them to take out all the treasures," I suggested. "Everything has gone and there are no bodies here either."

"Thank goodness. It does seem possible," Kareem agreed. "But what happened once the tomb was empty?"

Neither of us wanted to think too much about that one.

"Maybe they have only just finished and they let them go. Ramy is probably already back in Australia," I suggested lamely.

We decided to try and get some sleep. I was just dozing off when I heard a scratching sound. I tried to reach the torch without disturbing Kareem but he woke straight away.

"What's up?" he asked.

"I can hear something scratching," I replied.

"It's probably a rat," Kareem said, stating what I had already suspected.

"What if there are lots of rats?" I asked, thinking that would be almost more than I could cope with right now. Kareem shone the torch at the back wall and, sure enough, there was a pretty big rat scratching at the bottom of the wall.

"It's only one," Kareem said reassuringly. "I expect he got trapped like us when the dynamite went off."

"Well, there's nothing here for him to eat, I haven't even seen a beetle. I guess he's also thirsty," I replied, almost feeling sorry for him. Hopefully he would die of thirst before he was hungry enough to eye us up as his next meal.

We watched the rat for a while and then, suddenly, he disappeared.

"He's gone," I said, stating the obvious.

"But where?" Kareem asked. "If it's a solid wall of ostraca he can't have gone through it. There must be a hole there – even if it's a very small hole."

Kareem had brought his digging tool with him and he ran over to where we last saw the rat. He stabbed desperately at the wall where the rat disappeared. For a while, nothing happened. Then he let out a yell, as the tool went through near the floor. He worked at the hole for a while and then he said:

"Actually there is something other than limestone here. Where the rat went through it is like a join where limestone meets plaster. I think what we have here is an entrance from another tomb, or corridors to another tomb, which has been sealed over. Unfortunately that means I am going to have to deface the hieroglyphics to make a hole big enough for us to get through."

'That's the least of our worries,' I thought to myself. Kareem worked for several hours to make the hole bigger. It was slow and laborious and his hands were blistered and bleeding. I took a turn but didn't make much progress – still, I had to do something. We were relieved when our efforts finally produced a hole big enough to shine the torch through. We could see that there was a space behind it, which seemed to go for a few feet. Would there be anything beyond that, or were we completely wasting our time and energy?

After a few hours we turned off the torches and slept again. I was so thirsty as we were rationing ourselves to a few mouthfuls at a time and my stomach was rumbling with hunger. I couldn't decide what was worse – being thirsty, being hungry or being confined. The three together made for a very miserable and depressed human being. We tried to console each other with thoughts of "we'll soon be out of here" but we both knew our chances of finding way out, even through another tomb, were fairly remote.

When we awoke, stiff and sore, we returned to our hole in the wall with renewed vigour. As always happens after sleep, our optimism returned and with it our confidence in finding a way out. Kareem went for it like a man possessed. We watched the beautiful hieroglyphics falling away and eventually the hole grew to the size of a man's head. Another look with the torch confirmed that there did indeed appear to be another tunnel – but how far did it go? I took over for a while and then Kareem returned to the task. After a few hours the hole was big enough for us to step through – we had made it! I hugged Kareem with joy.

Grabbing the other torch and what was left of our water, we stepped through the hole.

What Lay Beyond

As we stood on the other side the torch flickered and died. Kareem was right about the storage life of batteries in Egypt! Fortunately the other one had hardly been used and I quickly turned it on to check our new surroundings. There was a long tunnel in front of us, quite low, with bare walls and of course completely dark. No beautiful stories were depicted on these walls. We set off along the tunnel, shining the torch this way and that as we went to see if there were any tunnels or chambers leading off it.

After about half an hour we found a tunnel off to the right. Which way go to? There was no way I was going to explore one on my own whilst Kareem took the other.

"I think we should keep going," I whispered.

"Why are you whispering?" Kareem asked "no-one is going to hear us. My guess is we should take the one to the right."

We headed off down the right-hand tunnel. It went for about four hundred metres and then came to a dead end.

"Maybe it led to another tomb," I said, not really caring. We retraced our steps and continued on our original path.

We must have walked for about three kilometres before I saw a shaft of light ahead of us. Kareem saw it at the same time and we looked at each other and whooped with delight. We hurried towards it, hoping against hope that we had found our way out. There were steps up to the light and we could see a gate barring our way – but there was daylight and, switching off the torch, we climbed the steps like two excited children.

We reached the gate and peered out. There was no sign of life – just sand and ruins.

"It looks like the old workman's village of Deir El Medina," said Kareem. "That was where the villagers who worked on the tombs lived - they stayed near the tombs when they were working and only went home for their days off."

"How are we going to get out?" I asked impatiently, shaking the steel gate to no effect.

"We may have to wait for someone to come along," Kareem replied patiently. "If I am right, this is only about ten minutes from the Antiquities Inspectorate and lies between the modern villages of Qurnet Murai and Sheikh Abd el Qurna. Also it is a tourist site, although we are obviously at the wrong end of it. I understand they only open the main street to the tourists so they do not come this far."

I sat down, exhausted. We were so close to freedom and yet we were still entombed. I took a drink of water and handed it to Kareem.

"Not more than a few mouthfuls left," he commented.

"We should shout for help," I suggested. It is very quiet and someone might hear us."

"It's worth a try," Kareem agreed "but our

taxi. The driver understood Luxor and we were soon leaving the village of Qurnet Murai. We farewelled our rescuers and our host, waving until they were out of sight. We must have looked a sight when we returned to the hotel, but fortunately Hamadi was not around and we were able to sneak into our room and shower. After that we fell into bed and into an exhausted sleep, which lasted until late in the afternoon.

When we awoke, safe and refreshed, we sat and talked about our ordeal. We knew we were very lucky to have survived. We also knew that the only person who would have any reason to bury us alive was Gahiji.

"He must know what has happened to Ramy," Kareem reasoned. "Otherwise he would have no reason to do us any harm? If it wasn't him who set off the dynamite then it must have been others involved with him. He is our only link to Ramy."

"Shall we go to the police?" I asked.

At that moment there was a knock on the door. It was Hamadi.

"Where have you been?" he inquired. 'Your friend, John Turner, is on the phone. He rang yesterday and I couldn't find you."

"Qurnet Murai," I called out, as I rushed down the hall to pick up the phone. John sounded relieved to hear my voice.

"I was starting to worry about you," he said.

"So you should," I retorted. "I have a lot to tell you but I can't say much now."

"It's my day off tomorrow. I'm not doing anything, how about I drive up there?"

"That would be great," I replied. "We'd love to see you."

Our next step was to contact the rental company. For this we needed Hamadi's help to translate. We told him the car had broken down and we had managed to get a lift to Qurnet Murai where we spent the night. We didn't want to go anywhere near Gahiji's house or for him to know we had escaped, so the best solution seemed to be to let the rental company think the car had stopped and for them to collect it. We could always rent another one later if necessary.

We spent the evening trying to make sense out of what we had discovered.

"My brother's St Christopher," said Kareem, pulling it out of his pocket and fastening it around his neck "means he was in the same tomb that we were in. We know that Yasmeen and he were probably taken because of her father's connection to the tomb, so it makes sense to believe they were the link to the kidnappers finding the location of it. That would explain why Yasmeen's father has also disappeared. They would have used Yasmeen as the bartering tool to get him to go to them and to reveal what he knew about the tomb. He must have taken them to it. But what happened to them afterwards?"

"I suppose," I said after a while "it rather depends on whether there was anything left in the tomb when they opened it. If it was empty, they would no longer be of any use to them, which probably explains the ransom demand. If, on the other hand, it was full of treasures, then they have obviously removed them all, and by the amount of well-worn tracks leading from the road to the tomb it would seem to me that they have indeed been busy doing just that. If that is the case, there is a slight chance they might have used Ramy, Yasmeen and her father to help them move it."

"Yes, yes," Kareem responded. "The tomb must have still been full of treasures – otherwise why would there be so many tracks? But what happened to them afterwards?"

We still didn't seem to be any closer to finding Ramy.

John Turner arrived early the next morning. I ordered some coffee and we went up to our room so we could speak in private. We quickly filled John in about our entombment and rescue.

"I'm just so glad you are safe," he said when we had finished, looking straight at me. "If you are right and the tomb had not already been robbed, then this is a very serious matter for the Egyptian authorities. They do not take kindly to someone removing their treasures and either keeping them for themselves or trying to sell them overseas. It seems to me it is unlikely they would want to make too many approaches in Egypt itself or word would get around that a new tomb has been robbed and that would be very dangerous for them. It is much more likely that the goods are to be shipped out of Egypt to an overseas buyer. They may even already be on their way.

I think now you should report it to the authorities in Cairo. They can then interview this Gahiji and maybe find something out about Ramy, Yasmeen and Masud. The fact that Egyptian treasures could be involved will certainly cause the authorities to take the search more seriously."

"The authorities don't seem to be getting anywhere," Kareem responded. "I just don't know if we should go to them or just pursue Gahiji ourselves."

"You know I can't advise you to do that, in my official capacity," replied John. "However, I wouldn't anyway. You were very lucky to escape this time, you may not be so lucky again if you go stirring things up. I think you should relocate to Cairo where you will be harder to find. Once you put in a report about Gahiji I can then approach them in my official capacity and exert more pressure on them to find out what Gahiji knows about
your brother."

By the time John left, it was settled. Kareem and I would return to Cairo tomorrow and lodge a complaint.

The next day we bade Hamadi farewell and thanked him for all his help. He was sorry to see us go but assumed we were returning to

Australia.

"Have a good trip," he said as we climbed into the taxi.

We booked into a small hotel in Cairo recommended by John and then made our way to the police station. A couple of hours later our story had been told, questions had been asked and we returned to our hotel, not at all confident that anything would come of it.

Some time later the police came to our hotel.

"You are required to come with us," they said. "The Ministry officials want to talk to you."

Feeling we were not being given any choice, we went out to their car and were whisked away to a large, old building in the centre of Cairo. Here we were interviewed separately and at some length. When we were finally put in a car and returned to our hotel we felt more like criminals than victims.

It was now time to ring my boss and try to explain why I was still in Egypt. However, he was not in any frame of mind to listen.

"I need you here, Anna. You have been gone far too long and I can't manage without you any longer. It is time you returned to your job."

I put the phone down somewhat disheartened. Part of me was ready to go home, I had to admit, but the other part wanted to support Kareem and to stay until we found out what had happened to the others. Reluctantly I told Kareem about my conversation with Jim.

"You must go, Anna," he said immediately. "I don't know how much longer I can stay myself. Your job is important and Jim has been very patient. Besides, it is dangerous for you here now. Much as I want you to stay with me, I know it is time for you to go back to Australia."

So it was decided, I would return to Australia and my job and leave Kareem to continue the search for his brother, at least for a while longer.

Before I left I went to visit Mrs Ahmose again and I took Kareem with me. She welcomed us warmly and was anxious to hear our news. Pili and Omar sat with us as we told them about finding the tomb and being blocked in. I told them my theory that Masud had led the tomb robbers to the secret tomb to save Yasmeen's life. Kareem showed her Ramy's St Christopher, which he now wore around his neck all the time and told her how he had found it in the tomb.

"We know he was alive up to that point, and hopefully Masud and Yasmeen also. Unfortunately, we still have no idea what has happened since."

Mrs Ahmose was amazed to hear about the secret tomb and, for Pili and Omar, it was the first they had heard of it.

"I can't believe you never told us," said Omar.

"Your father never wanted you to know. He

said it was better that way – he was convinced there was a curse on it and this way there was no temptation. In fact we had never spoken of it again from that day – I had forgotten it even existed."

I explained that I must now return to my job in Australia but that Kareem would stay on in Egypt a bit longer to look for them and he promised to keep in touch.

But before I left Egypt there was one more thing I wanted to do – visit the Pyramids. How could I leave without seeing them? They are one of the Seven Wonders of the World and the only one still surviving. Kareem and I headed out early the next morning to try and beat some of the tourist buses. As we approached in the taxi the pyramids appeared in front of us, above the road. A lone camel was standing in front of the pyramid closest to us, high above our heads, with his rider hunched over, almost asleep in the saddle. I quickly took a photo as we slowed down around the bend – to me that picture epitomised Egypt as I had imagined it before leaving Australia.

The carpark where the taxi stopped was enormous. Already several coaches were parked there and it was obvious that later in the day it would be packed. We walked across to the Khufu, or Great Pyramid and I was amazed at the size of it. Nothing can prepare you for the enormity of the pyramids – all the photos I had seen, the programmes on TV, none of them had conveyed the size of these icons. As we drew closer it seemed to become even more impressive. I took Kareem's photo with him standing in front of one of the stones – he only came up to about two-thirds of the height of it. We climbed up a few but there didn't seem much point in going any higher. "It is one hundred and thirty-seven metres high," Kareem informed me. Instead we clambered back down and walked around to the other large pyramids.

"Originally the pyramids were covered in limestone. Look at that one over there." He pointed to the pyramid of Kafre. "It still has its limestone peak, even though the limestone has fallen from the rest of it."

In the distance we could also see smaller pyramids, which apparently were built for wives and daughters of the Pharaohs. We had the option of climbing up to the doorway of the pyramid of Khufu and going inside. However, the thought of a very low, narrow tunnel after what we had just been through gave me goose-bumps. Instead we went into the Museum of the Solar boat, next to the pyramid of Khufu. It housed a huge wooden boat, some forty-three metres long. This boat had been found buried in one thousand, two hundred and twenty-four pieces alongside the pyramid, together with seven pairs of oars. It was to take the Pharaoh to the afterlife and all the parts had been carefully placed in a huge pit for his use. It had taken ten years to assemble. I chuckled to myself imagining the

Pharaoh trying to assemble it by himself!

All around us were camels and even horses for hire with the touters making a real nuisance of themselves, offering free photos on their camel, a cheap ride, a special experience. In reality, once a tourist took them up on their offer they were bullied into parting with a lot more money – either to do the return trip of even just to get off the camel. Not too many people will jump off a camel that is still standing.

We went across for a close-up look at the Sphinx. It was such a pity, I thought, that the nose had been blown off. It was still magnificent though.

"It is believed that King Tuthmosis IV had a dream in which the Sphinx offered him the Double Crown of Egypt if he would dig him out of the sand which had covered him – and that is exactly what happened." Kareem informed me.

From the Sphinx I couldn't help but notice how close civilisation had come to these great monuments.

"Once there was a tree-lined boulevard leading up to the pyramids," Kareem continued. "Now the shops are built nearly up to the Sphinx and the city seems to come right to its door."

I looked around – across to the pyramids there was just desert. To the front and right of the Sphinx were shops and a road. It seemed quite incongruous. For me though, nothing could detract from the grandeur and uniqueness of the Sphinx and the pyramids. It had been a dream come true to visit them and to see the true spirit of Egypt.

Before I left the next day, we called in to see John Turner at the Embassy. He told us that the authorities had picked up Gahiji and interviewed him. If he was surprised to hear that Kareem and I were alive, apparently he did not show it. He vehemently denied all knowledge of the tomb, of us, our entombment or of Ramy, Yasmeen and Masud.

John assured me that the authorities and the police would continue to keep an eye on him and to check out anyone he contacted.

Back in Australia

In the time I had been away a lot had happened. The leadership spill had taken place, as predicted, and Paul Keating was now the new PM. It was December 1991 and an election was not due until 1993. I always dreaded election times and was hoping it would not be called early. I also hoped it would be a short time between the calling of the election and the election date. It was always total chaos the minute the election was announced and long campaigns are hard on everyone. Jim would want to write to every constituent, help some of the other local candidates in marginal seats and every constituent with a problem would decide this was the right time to ask for help. Fortunately Jim's seat was fairly blue-ribbon but he was a stickler for doing the work to give himself every opportunity of being re-elected. I was rather pleased about that though, because if he lost his seat, I was out of work too.

My friend Sandra rang to tell me she was getting divorced. I wasn't surprised as I knew she had been unhappy for quite a long time but naturally she was very upset and I was glad to be around to give her some time and support. Sandra and I had been friends for years – we met when we worked for the same company – and she stayed over for a couple of nights. We talked until late, drank too much wine, laughed and cried, as best friends do. I told her more of my adventure in Egypt which helped to take her mind off her own problems for a while.

It soon felt as if my time in Egypt had been a dream – or, rather, a nightmare. I missed Kareem but catching up on my work after being away took up most of my time. He rang me every few days but the line was usually dreadful and the calls were short. I also heard from John Turner – he could fax me direct from the Embassy and he sent me brief updates. The police had interviewed Gahiji again but had not been able to get anything more out of him. We were certain he was not innocent so we could only assume he was very scared of the people he was involved with as he would not give up their names.

Then one evening when I was working late the phone rang and it was John.

"How lovely to hear from you, John."

"How are you Anna?" he asked.

"I'm fine," I replied "working all hours but otherwise good."

"Anna, this is not a social call I'm afraid. I'm sorry to bring you such bad news. There is no easy way to tell you this. It's Kareem, Anna, he's been found dead."

I felt as if the world was crushing down on me. It was hard to breathe.

"Anna, Anna, are you there? Are you okay?"

"Yes....yes I'm here" I managed to whisper. "What happened? How did they kill him? Have they arrested those responsible?"

"It wasn't murder, Anna. He just died. He was in his hotel room and it seems he had an aneurism in the brain. It could have been as a result of the knock on the head which led to his amnesia. The doctor said it could have happened at any time but it just burst and bled into his brain and he died very quickly. The hotel staff found him the next day. Anna, I'm so sorry. Is there someone I can call for you?"

I couldn't think straight.

"No, no..... I'll be fine. Thanks for letting me know, John," I managed to say. "I'm going now but I'll be in touch later."

"Will you be alright?" John wanted to know. "Are you sure there isn't someone you want me to call for you?"

"No, I'll be fine," I replied. "I just need some time to think."

"Call me if you need anything," John said, meaning it. "I've already contacted Kareem's mother and she is making arrangements for his body to be flown home."

I sat there stunned. I couldn't think straight. My mind wouldn't accept that Kareem was dead. How could he be when I had just got him back again? Surely this was just some awful prank, a nightmare I would soon wake up from. I couldn't believe that I would never see him again, not touch him or hold him. It wasn't fair. We had such a short time together. Then I thought of his mother. She had lost her husband, one son was missing and now this – her oldest son dead, killed whilst looking for his brother. Yes, killed, because if he hadn't taken the blow to the head over the ransom money he would still be alive.

The next few days passed in a daze. I went to see Kareem's mother and we cried together – two women locked in grief over the death of a man they both loved. The day of the funeral came and went – the funeral itself passed in a blur; many faces I didn't know, but everyone was very kind and sympathetic. The finality of watching the coffin being lowered gently into the ground was almost too much for me. I let out a moan and Kareem's mother squeezed my arm. I went back to the house with her for the wake but after about an hour I excused myself and hurried back home. As I bade my farewell Mrs Hazif hugged me tightly and begged me not to be a stranger.

As I cried myself to sleep that night – surprised I still had tears to shed – I came to a decision. I could not let his death go unavenged. I would return to Egypt and finish what Kareem had set out to do – find his brother. I would not let him die for nothing.

The next morning, however, common sense returned.

What was a woman alone in Egypt going to achieve? I was more likely to end up as just another missing persons' statistic – particularly if Gahiji or his friends heard that I was still asking questions. It was time to be a little smarter.

I had to try to work out where the

antiquities would have been taken. From the track marks it seemed a donkey and cart were used to transport them from the tomb back to the track that passed as a road. The tyre marks belonged to quite a large truck and, if the tomb was untouched when they found it, the treasures would be numerous. They would need to be taken to a large shed where they could be sorted and shipped out. They would probably have needed a couple of forty-foot containers. Where could the goods have been taken, involving many trips over many weeks, without attracting any attention?

I channelled my energy and grief into work. I spent long days at the office and came home exhausted but only slept for three or four hours. Sandra was great – she came around as soon as I called her and rang each day to see if I was okay. My spare time was spent trying to work out where the goods were being stored. I poured over maps of Egypt and the Valley of the Queens/Deir el Medina area. The latter was certainly quite deserted but there was nowhere big enough to store the goods without drawing attention. Eventually I came to the conclusion that they had to be somewhere out past Gahiji's house. If the track only led to his house and then on to the storage shed, there would be no reason for anyone to go out that way. Assuming there was enough space to turn a large truck and forty-foot container around, it would be possible to get the truck down there if it was driven carefully. From there the containers could be taken to Port Said or even Alexandria to be shipped overseas without causing any great interest. I called my good friend John Turner.

"John, I think they have to be holding the goods out past Gahiji's house. There must be a big shed out there and probably a couple of large shipping containers. Can you get the police or authorities to go out and take a look?"

"I guess that's possible," John replied. "I'll take a run out there with the local police and see if there is anything."

"I just hope they haven't already moved them," I responded.

As I put down the phone I thought how lucky I was that John would take me seriously and follow up on my idea. I waited impatiently to hear back from him, cursing the time difference.

It was almost midnight when John rang back.

"Well, you were right about the big shed out past Gahiji's, Anna" John told me. "And you'll be very pleased to know we have Ramy, Yasmeen and Masud. They are all alive and safe!"

"Oh my goodness" I exclaimed. "I can't believe it. You actually have them safe and well? That's such good news. I am so excited! If only Kareem were alive to hear those words."

"I know, Anna. But think of his mother's excitement when you tell her Ramy is alive."

"Oh, you are going to let me give her the news? That's wonderful."

"If you contact her now, you will be the first to tell her. We'll make our official call in a few minutes."

"Tell me more, John. Where were they found? What happened when you went to look for the shed?"

"Well, there were lots of tyre marks out past Gahiji's. He must have swept the road up to there because there were no tracks to his house. The shed was well hidden in amongst some hills. We crept up on them and when I realised there were only two men guarding them we decided to move in ourselves. They came quietly enough when they realised we had them at a disadvantage. Ramy, Yasmeen and Masud had been used as workers. Yasmeen and her father were cataloguing the treasures and Ramy was the muscle, being used to stack the goods into one of two forty-foot containers. Unfortunately, we just missed the containers – they took them out the night before. There were only a few items left in the shed, which they were cleaning up and cataloguing. I don't know what would have happened to them if we had gone in any later – they no longer had any use for them. I can only think they would have killed them to protect themselves.

Customs at the ports of Alexandria and Port Said were notified immediately and have arranged for searches of all containers leaving the ports. My guess is that they are already on the water on the way to their new overseas owners to be part of very expensive private collections. However, Customs will continue to monitor for any unusual shipments over the next couple of weeks, just in case they did not have ships already lined up for the containers."

Whilst I felt very sorry for the Egyptian government who had lost out on these important antiquities my main thought was that Ramy was still alive and that Yasmeen and Masud were also okay. How happy Mrs Hazif and Waleed would be!

"On the way back we picked up Gahiji. They have all been interviewed extensively but at this point none will admit that anyone else was involved. Gahiji has admitted that he had heard of the tomb from his father and it was he who had known about Masud's father and made inquiries about Masud. When he found he was involved in the antiques business we assume he then contacted Mohammed, whoever he is, to take the matter further. He obviously thought it was worth a visit to Cairo to check out Masud and his shop. Gahiji has made no admissions regarding you and Kareem and I don't think he is likely to do so. The authorities will continue to work on him to find out who this Mohammed is and who else was involved. Rashidi and Mosi were just the foot soldiers but they will also keep working on them to see if they know who Mohammed is, but at the moment they are denying all knowledge of him."

I hung up from John to make that important phone call to Ramy's mother. She was, of course, crying and laughing at the same time, so happy to know that at least one of her sons was coming back to her. After promising to go around and have a meal with them one day next week I put through a call to Yasmeen's mother. Again, there was much laughter and crying and Waleed was very grateful to me for making good use of the information she had passed on to me.

A few days later I had a call from Ramy's mother, inviting me for dinner. Apparently Yasmeen and Masud had returned to their home and Ramy, having visited his aunt and uncle, had arrived back in Australia. Yasmeen was to follow on in a couple of weeks. This would give her a chance to see Australia and meet Mrs Hazif.

It was over dinner that Ramy told us all about his exploits. He had already filled his mother in regarding Yasmeen and their courtship, their kidnapping and finding the secret tomb filled with treasures. Tonight he picked up the story from the point at which they had emptied the tomb.

Ramy's Story Continues

"The last of the treasures from the secret tomb had been loaded on the truck. Up until now we had not been involved in the unloading and didn't know where they were taking the treasures. We assumed Gahiji was helping Mosi unload. At this point I had grave concerns for our safety as I could see that once the tomb was empty we would no longer be needed. Masud and I had talked about it one night when Yasmeen was asleep and Gahiji was outside. We knew we needed a plan – we would have to find a way to escape before our usefulness was over. Neither of us could come up with much – our best chance seemed to be to wait until there was only one person guarding us, to overpower him and then make a run for it. Masud knew the area a little. His car would still be parked where he left it but Rashidi had taken the keys off him immediately. We had checked in the little house and could find no trace of them so he had obviously taken them away somewhere we would never find them. That ruled out making our escape in the car. Masud knew that Queen Hatshepsut's temple was somewhere over the hills behind us and that if we made it to there the chances were good there would be tour buses and tourists there and we would be safe. The only problem – and the reason why we had not tried it before – was they always had a gun with them. However we knew there would come a day when we would just have to take our chances.

After we had emptied the little cart in to the truck for the last time, Mosi took us back to the tomb, instructing us to cover the entrance and then wipe out our tracks back to the ravine. This might be our last chance, I thought, as I caught Masud's eye. He nodded to acknowledge he too knew this would have to be the moment we tried for escape. As we moved rubble to block the tomb I whispered to Yasmeen that something was going to happen and she should follow her father when he made a move. I made my way around behind Mosi, pretending to look for larger rocks. I found a good size one and crept up behind him. Clunk – and Mosi was on the ground, out cold.

"Run Masud, run Yasmeen," I called out as I went to grab his gun from under his robe.

They took off into the desert, just as Rashidi called out:

"Stop. Stop I shoot."

I left the gun and dived for a large rock and rolled behind it before springing to my feet and running. I heard the gun fire and I tried to dodge from side to side, as I had seen them do in the movies. The shot missed but Rashidi was coming after us fast and fired another shot in the direction of Yasmeen. Her father pushed her in front of him and the bullet hit his leg. They landed in a heap as another shot whizzed past me. By the time I had pulled Masud up Rashidi was on top of us. It turned out that when he got back to the truck it had a flat tyre and he had come back to get me to help him change it. Can you imagine such rotten luck? Anyway, to our surprise, he didn't shoot us – just bundled us back to the tomb where Mosi was just shaking his head and coming around. I helped her father back to the truck and Mosi brought up the rear, his gun at the ready in case we made another dash for freedom. After I changed the tyre, Masud was put in the truck and Yasmeen and I clambered into the donkey cart as usual. Yasmeen was very upset of course, but I told her it was a clean wound – the bullet had passed right through his leg – and that her father would be fine. I realised afterwards that we hadn't put much over the entrance to the tomb, nor removed our tracks.

When we got back to the house, Gahiji proceeded to clean up Masud's leg with disinfectant and some foul-smelling ointment. Not long after, Mohammed appeared and he was very angry with us.

"Look what you have done now," he said, waving his hand in Masud's direction. "We still have work for you to do. You - " he pointed at Yasmeen "and your father will need to catalogue the treasures ready for sale. And you -" he said pointing at me, "will load them into shipping containers. But now we have another use for you too. We need money to ship the containers and to pay for things until we get paid for the goods. Your family in

Australia can pay a ransom for you?"

I nodded vigorously and he chuckled.

"What luck it has been to have you along after all, eh Aussie?"

"How much do you think your family will pay for you?" he asked. I shook my head.

"One million dollars?" he suggested. I laughed.

"We do not have that much money. My mother has the house, nothing else."

"How about five hundred thousand?" I shook my head again.

"Well, how much do you think you are worth then?" Mohammed asked, starting to get frustrated. I decided it was time to make a suggestion.

"Two hundred and fifty thousand Australian dollars," I replied.

"Okay, give me the number and your mother's name," Mohammed demanded. There was no phone in the house in which we were kept prisoners so Mohammed left to make the ransom call.

When he returned he announced "Okay, your family think you are worth two hundred and fifty thousand dollars, that is good. Soon we will have enough money for our needs. Now, get some rest for tomorrow you start your new job."

Laughing loudly at his own joke, Mohammed took his leave.

The next day we were taken to a huge shed, further on from Gahiji's house. There we saw all the antiquities we had taken from the tomb, as well as two forty-foot shipping containers. Yasmeen and Masud then spent many weeks cataloguing the items. Masud's leg healed up okay. He was in quite a lot of pain at first and I would take the objects over to him to catalogue so he could work with his leg up. Then I would have to pack and load them into one of the two containers –either the USA one or the Australian one. I made a mental note of where the containers were to be sent.

Then not long after lunch on the fifth day Mohammed reappeared. He was obviously very happy.

"You are right," he said to me, slapping me on the back "your family have paid good money for your return. Well done, Aussie."

So that was how it came to be that Kareem was at the temple to hand over the ransom money. My poor brother – I cannot believe that he is dead. To know that he died trying to find me is both wonderful and sad."

We were all quiet for a few minutes, remembering Kareem's gallant effort to locate Ramy and bring him home. Our sadness was almost palpable.

"Anyway," Ramy continued "we finally filled the two containers and only a few special items remained. These had been put aside by Mohammed – I don't know if they were for his personal collection or whether he had another buyer. Yasmeen told me they were very fine pieces. We were just cataloguing them when the doors to the shed burst open and the

Egyptian police arrived. Only Rashidi and Mosi were there and they soon rounded them up and then the Australian Embassy guy came in. He introduced himself as John Turner and said how pleased he was to have found us. He told us that they had been looking long and hard to solve our disappearance.

We were taken back to Cairo for questioning and allowed to leave after making our statements. Yasmeen and Masud went home whilst I had to go to the Australian Embassy to see John Turner and make another statement. He seemed very pleased that we were all safe and well and told me he had been keeping in close contact with you, Anna. Then he told me about my father and Kareem. I couldn't take it in at first. It didn't seem possible that both of them could be dead whilst I had come through all this unscathed.

The Embassy arranged for a room in a hotel for me and I can't tell you how wonderful it was to have a hot shower and a comfortable bed. Whilst we had not been harmed and had sufficient food and somewhere to sleep and bathe, we were kept in very primitive conditions. Although they did not treat us badly, as long as we behaved and did as we were told, the threat of violence and the ever-present guns kept us on edge. That night I slept deeply and contentedly. The next day I went to see my aunt and uncle to let them know I was okay and they made a big fuss of me and prepared a huge feast. Then I went over to meet Yasmeen's mother. Mrs Ahmose made me very welcome and Yasmeen looked so different after a good night's sleep free of stress.

"I love Yasmeen, you know" he said quietly, looking at his mother. "She is going to come to Australia to see what it is like and to meet you, Mum, and then we are going to be married."

"I hope you are not going to live in Egypt?" Mrs Hazif said in alarm.

"No, Mum," Ramy replied, "I have had quite enough of Egypt for the time being and Yasmeen has agreed to come and live in Australia, as long as she sees her parents regularly."

Mrs Hazif sighed a big sigh of relief. She had been through a horrendous time, losing her husband, not knowing what had happened to Ramy and then Kareem's untimely death. She did not look as if she could take much more.

"I knew that Gahiji was involved somehow," I said. "He came across as shifty when Kareem and I went out there. That's why I thought there might be somewhere to store the treasures out that way."

"I'm glad you had that hunch. If it wasn't for you getting John Turner to send the police out there, I don't know what would have happened to us once the last of the antiquities had been documented and packed. Another day and ...." Ramy shuddered thinking about their likely end.

I also thought they would probably have been shot once they were no longer needed for anything and it seemed we only got there on time by the skin of our teeth. Thank goodness I had made the call to John – I don't think I could have lived with myself if I had found out later that they had discovered their bodies in an empty shed near Gahiji's house. To think that we had been at the house where they had been kept overnight and not had any idea. If only we had realised, seen some evidence of Ramy's existence there, perhaps Kareem would be alive today. If we had been back in Australia and I had been with him when the clot had burst, maybe he would have survived. Without the stress, maybe it would not have burst at all. I shook myself out of my thoughts and back to the present. Ramy was telling his mother about Yasmeen. He was clearly besotted with her and it seemed, she with him.

"How soon will Yasmeen arrive?" I asked.

"She is coming next month" Ramy replied. "She needs some time with her family and she will return to work for a while and then she will come to me."

The rest of the evening passed quite easily, with the conversation turning to the places Ramy wanted to take Yasmeen to in Australia. As I took my leave at the end of the night Mrs Hazif hugged me warmly.

"Thank you for bringing Ramy back to me," she whispered. "I am just so sorry that we have both lost our Kareem."

Fate's Next Twist

My life soon fell back into a pattern – work, home, going out with friends and more work. I grieved for Kareem and cried myself to sleep regularly. The slightest thing could set me off – a movie on the TV, an ad depicting a couple enjoying a sunset, an advertisement for a holiday in Egypt showing the pyramids and temples. By day I managed to push these thoughts out of my mind – work was so busy and required all my concentration, but at night my thoughts wandered and they always returned to Kareem.

John Turner rang to let me know that Gahiji, Mosi and Rashidi were due to stand trial in a few days' time. They had not revealed the names of the people they worked for and were saying very little. Gahiji had admitted that he had learned of the tomb from his father on his deathbed, but that he had died before he could tell him where it was. He had told Mohammed, who had traced Masud and visited his shop. However Gahiji claimed that he did not know Mohammed's surname or where he was. I was angry; I wanted to see justice done. I needed to see the man who had hit Kareem stand trial for his death. None of the three arrested had admitted to hitting him and grabbing the ransom money, nor had they put anyone else in the frame for it. I wanted to see someone punished for Kareem's death and for trying to bury us alive but as John pointed out to me, proving any connection with either of these events was going to be almost impossible.

"Gahiji is not going to admit to sealing off the tomb's entrance and you cannot prove that he did it. You didn't see him and are only assuming he was the one who set off the dynamite. Likewise no-one will admit to stealing the ransom money and even if they did, it cannot be proved without a doubt that Kareem's aneurism was definitely caused by that blow to his head. The Egyptian authorities take the stealing of Egypt's antiquities very seriously. They will come down very hard on these three perpetrators and they will receive very stiff sentences. It is much better for you to leave it to them to punish them. Otherwise you will spend a lot of time back in Egypt for the trial, waste a lot of money and at the end you will probably not achieve anything."

Reluctantly I accepted the wisdom of these words. The trial was likely to be quite a way off. Every effort would be made to find out who was behind all this. Obviously it was none of the three already arrested. They would be interviewed over and over again and coerced into giving up the name of the mastermind in exchange for a more lenient sentence. Only time would tell if any of them would yield to this type of interrogation.

It was another month before John rang again to let me know the trial had started.

"Tomorrow they begin the preliminaries and soon we will know what is to become of the three prisoners. They have not given up any names so far."

"Please let me know how things progress, John" I pleaded.

"Actually, that's going to be a bit hard, Anna. You see, I will not be in Egypt much longer. I have resigned my posting and I'm coming back to Australia tomorrow."

I was taken by surprise at this news.

"But I thought you loved your job in Egypt," I exclaimed.

"I have enjoyed the experience immensely," John replied. "I'm not just resigning from the post in Egypt though. I'm leaving the service altogether. I want a change of direction. Can I take you out to dinner when I return and tell you all about it?"

"Yes, that would be nice. Why don't you call me when you are settled?"

After I put down the phone I spent the rest of the evening wondering why John would want to quit the Department of Foreign Affairs. I also had to examine my own feelings. I was feeling very pleased at the thought of seeing John again. How could I feel this way so soon after losing Kareem? Eventually I decided it was nothing more than looking forward to seeing a friend again. It couldn't be more than that, surely.

It was only a matter of days before John rang. We arranged to meet in the City at an Italian restaurant at Darling Harbour. John was already there when I arrived and had picked a lovely table overlooking the water. He kissed me lightly on the cheek and pulled out my chair.

"It's great to see you again, Anna" he said.

We chatted idly for a while about his journey and he told me how much he was enjoying being back in Australia.

"There's no city in the world like Sydney," he declared as a paddle-steamer pulled out from the wharf in front of us, lit up like a Christmas tree and full of happy tourists. "Cairo is an amazing experience but it's not somewhere you would want to spend the rest of your life."

We sat quietly, gazing at the lights of the buildings reflected in the water. There were blue, red and white lights, even some green and amber, shining down on the yachts in the Marina in front of us. We could see the old South Steyne ferry moored across the other side of Darling Harbour, proudly lit up in its new life as a floating restaurant.

"So what are you going to do now you are back in Australia and out of Foreign Affairs?" I asked.

"I'm planning to have a couple of months off and catch up with old friends. Then I'll look around. I don't really want to work for anyone else again so I may start up my own business. Who knows, I might even go into antiques!"

We both laughed at this and I asked him if he had heard any more about the trial.

"It is proceeding slowly, as things do in Egypt. I still have contacts in the Department of course and they will keep me updated. I have no doubt that they will all go away for a very long time."

The rest of the evening passed pleasantly and we finished the night with a stroll around Darling Harbour.

"When can I see you again, Anna?" he asked as the time came to say goodnight. "I know you are still grieving for Kareem but I do enjoy your company."

I suggested he ring me in a few days and we could catch up for a drink.

Over the next few weeks I saw quite a lot of John. He didn't seem to be in any hurry to go back to work. He had an apartment in the city, which so far I had avoided going to see. I enjoyed his company - he was funny, thoughtful and generous - but I didn't want to take our friendship any further. John didn't push me, but I knew he was hoping our relationship would soon go to the next level. I liked John a lot, but I was still grieving for Kareem and knew I was not ready for another relationship yet.

Eventually the news came from Cairo that I had been waiting to hear. The trial was over and the sentences handed down. Gahiji, who was considered to be a minor player, was given seven years. Rashidi and Mosi were each given fifteen years. They never revealed the names of those they worked for and steadfastly denied any knowledge of anyone called Mohammed, even though it could have resulted in a lighter sentence. It seemed those master-minding the operation had them well and truly frightened and although the investigation would be ongoing, it was not looking very likely they would ever be found.

To celebrate, John threw a party and so at last I went to his apartment. He had invited a few friends over he wanted me to meet. When I arrived at the address he had given me in Castlereagh Street I pressed the button to his apartment and was let into a very smart foyer. The lift took me up to the tenth floor and No.9 was around to the right from the lift. When John opened the door I was totally unprepared for the level of affluence of his apartment. It was quite magnificent, with a huge picture window giving a wonderful view of the city lights. There were five other couples already there enjoying drinks and the view.

"Wow, this is some apartment," I whispered in his ear. "I didn't realise what I was missing."

John just grinned and poured me a huge gin and tonic before taking me to see the two spacious bedrooms and the huge ensuite and main bathroom.

"You have done well for yourself."

The kitchen was state-of-the-art with a laundry off the back of it.

"This must set you back a packet."

"After two years in Cairo I figured I deserved a bit of comfort," was John's response.

I left my coat in the spare bedroom and prepared for a very pleasant evening. As the night drifted on, John put some dancing music on and invited me to dance. I felt his arms tighten around me and I let myself fall into the rhythm. It was very enjoyable to be held again and to melt into the music whilst gazing out at the light show below. The other guests were interesting. Only one person was someone John had worked with from the Department of Foreign Affairs, a man called Henry Whitehouse. A quiet, bespectacled man in his early forties, he and his wife, Margarita, talked to me about my experience in Egypt and wanted to know about being trapped in the secret tomb. They were quite amazed to hear my story first-hand. Henry had not been to Cairo but was fascinated to hear my insights into the city. We talked at length.

"It was quite odd that they never caught up with the containers full of treasures," he mused. "It was an extremely busy time at the ports when they were supposed to be shipped out. They must have had it all organised well in advance and managed to slip them through Customs by bribing one of the officials."

At this point John cut in and whisked me away for more dancing.

The other couples were friends whom John had known from Uni. Two of the guys, Peter and Graeme were lawyers with well-known Sydney firms. Their wives were very smartly dressed and were stay-at home mums. Both had a live-in nanny to help with the children and enjoyed a very pampered, leisurely life by my standards. His other two friends from Uni were female. Pamela, was in Public Relations and was quick to tell me she was divorced, no children and loved her work. The other girl, Julie, was a high-school teacher. All had travelled extensively so were very interesting to talk to and Julie and Pamela often holidayed together. Although she didn't mention her personal life, I understood Julie had never been married.

When all the guests had left, it seemed natural that I should stay on and help clear up. When the last glass was washed and put away John pulled me into his arms again and I didn't hesitate as his lips came down on mine. His kisses were hard and demanding but they lit a fire within me that I couldn't control.

The next morning whilst John was in the shower I went in to the spare room to retrieve my bag and coat. As I turned to leave the fax machine started up and made me jump. Without thinking I went over to it, so used to answering its call. The words 'The eagle has landed safely' jumped out at me and, intrigued, I let my eyes run across the rest of the text. 'Meet me outside Central Station opposite the youth hostel at one o'clock and we can finalise our deal'.

I suddenly realised I was snooping and pulled myself up quickly. I hadn't meant to read someone else's mail, it just sort of happened. I decided I would pretend I hadn't seen it. Over coffee I asked him what his plans were for the day.

"Oh, nothing much. A bit of business," he replied "but I'll be back by the time you finish work. Why don't you come over and I'll cook you dinner."

He nuzzled the back of my neck and my legs went weak.

"That would be lovely," I whispered, my voice hoarse.

I couldn't help musing over the fax I had seen as I went through the day. What sort of business deal was John involved in? He hadn't mentioned doing any business – he had seemed quite happy to enjoy some free time. And what did Henry mean about the Customs official? Presumably the authorities would have questioned everyone who was on duty on the nights they thought the goods would have been shipped and anything strange would have been reported.

That evening John cooked me a lovely meal – salmon in garlic and white wine, baby potatoes and a green salad. This was followed by a strawberry cheesecake and icecream and coffee with liqueur. Over dessert I asked him how his day had gone.

"Oh, pretty good," he replied "how was yours?"

"Not bad." I answered. "With the changes to Social Security we are getting quite a few of those inquiries now - makes a change from immigration anyway. Did your business today go okay?" I asked.

John's eyes narrowed as he looked at me quizzically. I could see he was wondering if I had seen the fax he had received that morning. I gazed innocently into his eyes.

"It was fine," he said and with that he changed the subject by standing up to clear the dishes. I decided I was being paranoid. After all, what could he possibly be involved in that was not on the up and up. I pushed the little feeling of uncertainty away and enjoyed the rest of the evening.

I don't know what got into me the next morning when he was in the shower and I started to make the bed and saw a bulging briefcase sticking out from under the bed. I pulled it out and opened it – it wasn't locked. Inside were wads of one hundred dollar bills! I stared at it for a moment – there must have been thousands of dollars in it. Then I quickly closed it and pushed it further under the bed and finished pulling up the sheets – my head reeling. When John came out of the shower I tried to act normally but I left as quickly as I could to gather my thoughts.

Of course, it could be perfectly legitimate. When he left the Department he could have had long-service leave payable and might have drawn it out to put it in a different Bank account today. Surely he wouldn't leave it unlocked if it was not legitimate? But that was more than long-service leave – he must have been putting all his money into a different Bank. But why wouldn't he have asked for a cheque? There must be a perfectly logical explanation, I thought but - try as I might - I couldn't come up with one. I couldn't wait for Friday to come when I would stay overnight again and could see if the briefcase was still there.

As soon as John went for his shower I looked under the bed. The briefcase was still there! Would it still be full of money? I flicked it open as quickly as I could and, sure enough, there was the money. What was going on? I couldn't believe that anyone would have a legal stash of money that big under the bed – despite Malcolm Fraser's suggestion when he was Prime Minister.

Over the next few days I wrestled with this problem, but came no closer to working out a solution in my head. This put quite a strain on my relationship with John. When I was with him I couldn't believe he could do anything wrong. When I was away from him my brain went into overload. I had to get this sorted - and quickly - before John sensed something was wrong.

Hard Decisions

Mrs Hazif rang me to say that Yasmeen had arrived in Australia and asked me if I would come for dinner to meet her. Of course I said I would be delighted and it was arranged for the following Thursday night. I was excited to finally be meeting the famous Yasmeen.

Ramy opened the door and gave me a hug. His mother was standing behind him and kissed me warmly. Then Ramy introduced Yasmeen. She was indeed as beautiful as Ramy had described her and obviously as much in love with him as he was with her. It was wonderful to see the love in their eyes as they gazed at each other across the table.

"How is your father, Yasmeen?" I inquired.

"Oh, he is good." she replied. "He is just so happy that we are both safe and to be back with my mother and brothers. Life is just so much more precious when you have looked death in the face."

I nodded my agreement.

"He can't stop talking about the beauty of the objects we handled though. To touch items of such splendour, as an antique dealer, and then not to see them again, is very hard – and for me too. He is hoping to get back the golden collar and the dagger. They were amongst the items still left in the shed and they were taken along with the other items as evidence. Now that the trial is over he thinks they may be returned to him. Even though they too were plundered from the tomb originally they had been in his possession for a very long time. He hopes the authorities may look on it as a little reward for what we have been through and for bringing at least three of those involved to account. They couldn't believe that my father would have known of the tomb for all those years and never did anything about it or told anyone else.

He went to the trial every day you know. He was hoping that one of them would crack and divulge the names of those who were really responsible. He was very disappointed that nothing further came out of the trial. He looked all around the court to see if Mohammed would turn up to watch the proceedings but he never showed."

I asked Yasmeen what she thought had happened to the two containers.

"It is hard to say. We did hear them identified as the container going to the US and the one going to Australia. If they had a ship lined up to take the containers straight on they would have got away. Once Customs were notified, I cannot see how they could have got through, although of course bribery is a very big part of everyday life for us in Egypt. It is not impossible that someone would have been offered a large sum of money to look the other way, but I'm sure the government officials themselves would have been there every day."

After that the talk turned to the wedding, which both Ramy and Yasmeen wanted to take place as soon as possible. Naturally Yasmeen wanted to be married in Egypt and so a date was settled on in April and Mrs Hazif was looking forward to her first trip to Egypt since she left there as a child. I knew financially it was going to be hard for the family. The ransom money had not been recovered and Mrs Hazif had mortgaged the house to raise it. She had friends who owned a shop who had promised her a job and she was going back to work for the first time in twenty-five years. Ramy was going to try and help her but of course he now had his own life to carve out. Fortunately there had been a small insurance policy on Mr Hazif's life which had enabled her to pay part of the mortgage off and to pay for her and Ramy's trip to Egypt for the wedding. Kareem had also saved a reasonable sum whilst living at home which was also put back into the mortgage.

"It has been so lovely to meet you, Yasmeen," I said as I took my leave. "I'm sure you and Ramy will be very happy together."

"Thank you," she replied. "I am so sorry that you lost Kareem. You must be very sad. We will send you an invitation to the wedding – you can stay with us. I hope you will come but of course we will understand if you never want to return to Egypt."

I hadn't mentioned John Turner, apart from saying in passing that he was back in Australia and we had caught up a couple of times. How could I explain how I had taken up with someone else so soon after Kareem's death? I couldn't explain it to myself, let alone to Kareem's family. Life goes on, but in my case, it was moving forward a little too fast!

When the wedding invitation came I was of two minds whether to accept or decline. I could just scrape up the airfare and Waleed had sent a handwritten note asking me to stay with them for a few days. It would be nice to see her again and to represent Kareem at his brother's wedding. I showed the invitation to John, which as usual was extended to "Anna and friend."

"If you want to come, I'll tell them about you. I'm sure they will understand."

"No thanks," John replied a little off-handedly. "I don't think it's appropriate for me to attend under the circumstances and, to tell the truth, I'm not very keen to return to Egypt so soon after leaving."

I thought about asking Sandra to come with me but in the end I caught a flight back to Egypt with Mrs Hazif and Ramy. They were very excited of course, whilst I was just uneasy. The thought of returning to the place of Kareem's death was unsettling – there were so many memories in Cairo, both good and bad and I was not at all sure it had been a good idea to return. In the end though I decided just to concentrate on the wedding, imagine I was anywhere in the world but Egypt and think about returning to Australia and John as soon as it was over.

Yasmeen and Waleed were at the airport to meet us. They had arranged accommodation nearby for Ramy and his mother, in a small hotel which was within walking distance of their home. On the journey from the airport the heat, the chaos of the roads and the never-ending honking of horns felt like it was closing in on me. I was glad when we arrived at the Ahmose house and Waleed served ice-cold tea in the darkened living room.

"It is lovely to see you again, my dear," she said. "It must be very hard for you to come back here." I nodded and sipped my tea. "As soon as you have finished your tea, you must lie down for a while," she suggested, much to my relief. As soon as I could I escaped to my room and within minutes of lying down I went into a deep sleep.

That evening Mr Ahmose, along with Omar and Pili returned from the shop. The boys seemed pleased to see me and it was great to finally meet Masud. I was feeling much better after my rest and Masud greeted me enthusiastically.

"You saved our lives – if it wasn't for you being so sure there was a storage shed out past Gahiji's, our usefulness would have been outlived and we would be dead. How can I ever thank you enough?"

"It was just a lucky hunch," I laughed. "You have to thank John Turner from the Australian Embassy and the Egyptian police who were prepared to act on a woman's intuition."

He hugged me and planted a kiss on both cheeks.

"Come, we must drink to our good health," he said, pouring me a large glass of wine.

Whilst I drank my wine I had the chance to assess Masud. He was shorter than Waleed and seemed to have put on any weight he might have lost whilst he was held captive, as his suit fitted him well. He walked with a slight limp, which I assumed was from the bullet wound. Pili had his nose and eyes, I thought and Omar has his mouth. He had a long moustache which he had twirled at the ends to make them stiff and straight and dark eyebrows that met in the middle of his nose. He noticed me looking at his moustache and said:

"What do you think of it, eh? I have always wanted a moustache and I had the chance to grow one whilst we were held captive. I don't think Waleed likes it very much though, do you dear?"

"It tickles," was all that Waleed was prepared to say.

Yasmeen returned then from settling Ramy and her mother-in-law to be into their accommodation. She and Ramy had lots to talk about after being separated for the past few weeks. Tomorrow she would be a married woman and would soon be leaving Egypt for Australia, as soon as her visa came through. Yasmeen had a lively couple of hours with us before we all went around to the hotel to join Ramy and his mother for a meal there. Although I enjoyed the evening immensely, I wasn't sorry when it was time to return to the house.

"You go and get some rest Anna," Waleed said as soon as we returned to the house. "Sleep well, tomorrow will be a big day for us all."

The wedding was to be held late the next afternoon. Yasmeen, Mrs Hazif and Waleed were having their hair done, but I declined to join them and decided to have a quiet morning and then do my own hair. Ramy was similarly at a loose end and we decided to go to the palace of King Farouk. Ramy had been there before when he first arrived in Cairo. "It seems a hundred years ago since I was here last" he said as we wandered around the huge collection of guns, knives and china which King Farouk had received as presents. They were set out in glass cupboards in wonderfully artistic displays. Afterwards we walked around the gardens, lined with canons. Here we talked about Kareem and Ramy told me how much it would have meant to him to have his older brother there at his wedding. He recalled memories from their childhood and how Kareem had always looked out for him.

"I am not surprised he devoted himself to finding me. He always took his responsibilities seriously. Once he had promised our parents he would find me, he was not going to stop until he did."

I asked Ramy what had happened once the police had located them in the shed.

"We were taken straight to the police station, where we gave a statement covering everything that had happened to us from the time Yasmeen and I were seized. Then I was taken to the Australian Embassy. Yasmeen and Masud were interviewed by the government officials concerned with looking after Egyptian treasurers."

"Did John Turner look after you at the Embassy?" I inquired.

"Yes, I had to wait a while for him to arrive, but then he interviewed me himself and took me to the hotel they had chosen for me."

"When you say you had to wait for him, why didn't he accompany you from the police station?"

"He said he had something to attend to," Ramy replied "Yasmeen told me later she saw him interviewing Gahiji. She said he was really laying down the law to him. I think he was trying to find out who he was working for, but as you know, none of them gave up the identities of anyone else involved. We only know there was someone called Mohammed – but of course nearly every second person in Egypt is called Mohammed in one of the many versions of the spelling of it!"

By now it was time to return to the house to help prepare for the wedding. Ramy went back to the hotel to spend his last couple of hours as a single man with his mother and I lent a hand in the Ahmose household.

The wedding was a grand affair with over two hundred guests. Yasmeen was dazzling in her bejewelled wedding dress. The white of the dress against her long, black hair and strong features was stunning. The service in the local Church was perfect, even if I couldn't understand the words. The reception, held in the village square, was something I will always remember. Large tables were set out laden with food prepared by the women. Everyone had helped – I had cut up fruit and bread – and everyone was in a good mood. The weather was perfect – the sun shone so brightly we had been glad of the coolness inside the Church for the service. Now it was a warm and balmy evening with just the hint of a breeze. As the night wore on the stars were there in their thousands, as if sending down a blessing on the happy couple from above. There was much laughter and lots of dancing. Masud insisted on dancing with both Mrs Hazif and myself. Watching Ramy and Yasmeen I couldn't remember ever seeing a happier couple and I just prayed that, after all they had been through, theirs would be a long and happy marriage. Later that night we waved them off on their honeymoon by the Red Sea.

The next day I caught my flight back to Australia with Mrs Hazif. We talked most of the way about the wedding and a mother's hopes that she would soon be a grandmother.

When I arrived home there was a message on the answering machine from John. 'Can't wait to see you – hope everything went well in Egypt.'

I didn't ring him straight away, I needed some time to step back and think. I was pleased he hadn't been at the airport to meet me. Going to Kareem's brother's wedding, with his mother, was very hard. Knowing I was already involved with someone else was even harder. Everything was happening so fast I needed time to adjust to it. I sat in the garden in the sun and drifted.

I was woken by the phone.

"Shall I come to you or will you come over here?" John wanted to know.

"I still have some washing to do – how about I come over to you tonight?" I hedged.

"Okay – I'll cook" he replied. "How was the wedding?"

"It was beautiful – Yasmeen looked amazing and they were both so happy."

"I'm glad you enjoyed it," John said. "It must have been hard with so many memories of Kareem."

"It was. I just need today to get my head around it."

"I do understand," John said sympathetically. "Really I do. I'll see you tonight."

We had a lovely evening and John was very attentive. I think he really had missed me! He cooked chicken and pasta in white wine and cream. We had a bottle of good champagne and a Sarah Lee chocolate dessert. This was the first time I had dated a man who could prepare a meal – it was quite a change!

"What have you been doing in my absence?" I asked him.

"Not a lot," he replied. "I spent a day at

Bondi Beach and another at Balmoral. It's not quite as much fun on your own though."

He made no mention of looking for work or of any business deals. When we turned in for the night our lovemaking was passionate yet tender and I fell asleep wrapped in his arms. No wonder I had fallen for this man.

I returned to work after this brief trip feeling more tired than before I left. As usual, things were full on and I had no time to think about how I felt about John or how he was able to maintain such an extravagant lifestyle without any signs of seeking employment.

The following Saturday we spent the day together. We wandered around Circular Quay, watching the ferries coming and going, the tourists wandering around and listening to the buskers. John said he would cook dinner so we went back to his apartment. He was in the middle of cooking when he realised he had forgotten to buy the wine.

"I'll just pop downstairs and get some."

"I can go if you like," I offered.

"No, sit down and enjoy the view – just keep an eye on the pan and I'll be back in a shake."

As he headed out to the lift the phone rang. I let it ring – I knew the answering machine would take it. It was a man's voice with a thick accent – he sounded Egyptian to me.

"The shipment has arrived. Please arrange to clear it on Monday."

The message sent a chill down my spine – could it be that John was somehow involved with bringing the antiquities into Australia? Before I could give it much thought he was back with the wine. I didn't mention the call – I saw him glance over to the flashing light and then ignore it, but he was edgy all though our meal. When I came out of the shower the light had gone off so John had taken his message and seemed much more relaxed. What would he do next?

Sunday morning I had arranged to meet some girlfriends for lunch and I was relieved to have an excuse to get away early. I needed time to think. My head was spinning and my mind certainly wasn't on our conversation over lunch. I rang John afterwards and told him I had a throbbing headache (which was sort of true) and I was going straight home to lie down.

By Monday morning I had made some headway with my thoughts. I had recalled that Gahiji had a brother, Rohmald, living in Australia. Maybe there was a link there. I spoke to Jim and told him what I was thinking. He gave me his full support and suggested I contact Customs. First I rang the police officer I had spoken to in Egypt. Fortunately he remembered me and was able to give me Gahiji's surname – El-Masri. I then rang the Parliamentary Liaison officer in Customs. Di and I had spoken many times and were quite friendly. I explained to her briefly what had happened in Egypt and told her I had a feeling there would be a container coming through from Egypt being sent to a Mr Rohmald El-Masri – or a John Turner. I believed it contained the missing Egyptian antiquities. Di thanked me for the call and promised to pass on the information to the Customs officers at Sydney. She assured me they would look out for it and arrange for a search if it turned up. I hung up the phone feeling like a traitor. Did I really believe that the man I had been seeing for the past weeks was capable of stealing from the Egyptian government?

Later that day, Di called me back.

"We have found your container," she said. "It was addressed to Rohmald El-Masri and marked as containing souvenirs. However when the officers opened it and looked behind the couple of cheap souvenirs at the front, they were blown away by the quality of the treasures it contained. They resealed it and waited for the agent listed on the paperwork to come and clear it – John Turner. He has been taken in for questioning. Police and Customs officers then went to Rohmald's address in Western Sydney and arrested him. So far he has admitted he knew the shipment was coming but maintains that he was only doing a favour for his brother, Gahiji. He had nothing to do with the actual removal of the items from the tomb, nor their shipment from Egypt. He had just been told a container full of souvenirs was being sent to Australia and they needed to use his name and address until their contact could claim them."

I could hardly speak – although I had suspected that somehow John was involved, I hadn't wanted to believe it and was hoping and praying that I had been mistaken.

"What did John say?" I managed to gasp.

"We haven't interviewed him yet."

"Can I come in to the station? You see, he's a very good friend of mine."

"In that case," Di replied "they will probably need to take a statement from you too."

I arrived at the police station, dreading the news I was about to receive.

"John Turner is still being interviewed," I was told. "Come in and we'll take your statement."

I didn't want to make a statement until I heard John's story. Not that I was going to pervert the course of justice, but I would feel better telling my story if I knew he had already confessed to whatever he was involved in.

"I need to ring my boss and let him know what has transpired" I countered.

I rang Jim and he congratulated me on helping to track down the missing antiquities.

"I'll put out a press release straight away" he said, in true political form.

As I returned to the front desk, John was being brought out of another office. He mouthed "I'm sorry" as they led him away and I knew my worst fears had been confirmed.

I learned the story from the Customs officer who had accompanied John to the police station. It seemed that when John had the opportunity to talk to Gahiji immediately after his arrest he had demanded to know the name and contact number of his boss. He told Gahiji in no uncertain terms that unless the containers had already left the country there was no way they would be able to get them out without his help. He only had a few minutes to make a decision and Gahiji opted to give John the information. John then contacted this Mohammed who admitted they had not been able to get the containers away that night. John then told him his only chance of getting the containers out now was with his help. He could tell them when the search was called off and how to slip them through Customs. Once the first container arrived safely in America, Rohmald had paid him his first commission. The second one was due once he had cleared the container in Australia.

Later, after I had made my statement, I was allowed a few minutes with John and he again apologised.

"I have been a fool," he told me. "I have never done anything dishonest in my life, but I saw an opportunity to earn some really big money and I went for it. I was able to make contact with Mohammed thanks to Gahiji and I told him that, for a price, I could help him get the containers out.

We waited a couple of weeks and then I arranged for the container to America to be sent as my personal effects. Not much notice is taken of the goods of an Embassy official relocating. I kept in touch with my contact in

Customs and when I knew the Customs operation had been stepped down, I gave them the all clear to ship the one to Australia, offering to clear it through Customs in Australia myself. I thought a Caucasian like myself would draw less suspicion that someone of Egyptian background such as Rohmald. I have given them Mohammed's phone number so hopefully they will be able to track him down and he too will be put away. Through my greed and stupidity, I have lost my reputation, self-respect and, worse of all, you."

He looked up at me hopefully but I could not meet his gaze. The man I had put my faith in had let me down badly and I knew it was the end of our relationship. John would be going to prison for some time and when he came out he would have no job and no prospects. Most of all, he was not the man I thought I knew and had fallen in love with. I walked out of the police station feeling totally shattered.

I was consoled by the fact that Mohammed would be jailed for masterminding the theft and that the Egyptian government would have one container full of antiquities returned to them. They might even be able to track the American one from information from Mohammed, although I doubted he would admit to that one. However, it transpired that this was not to be. When Customs rang Mohammed's number he had already left the address and the new owner did not know where he had gone. Although he was able to give them Mohammed's surname he managed to slip through the net, probably with a new name. It was unlikely the authorities would ever catch up with him.

Rohmald himself was questioned extensively but eventually they had to let him go. Even though John testified that he had paid him the money, there was nothing to link him with the theft, apart from his relationship with his brother. He steadfastly claimed that he knew nothing about the antiquities and was only guilty of paying a debt on behalf of his brother. He maintained he knew nothing of the container his brother had addressed to him.

As for me, I silently vowed that men were definitely off the agenda – work would again be my salvation. However, a little nagging voice inside my head suggested that, like the Sphinx, one day I might lift my head high and rise up out of the sand once more.

About the Author

Rita Lee Chapman was born in London and moved to Australia in her early twenties. It was only when she retired to the Sunshine Coast in Queensland that she wrote her first novel 'Missing in Egypt'.

"This fulfils a lifelong ambition for me. In primary school I wrote long stories but since then my writing had been restricted to business correspondence and letters home to my family! Having read repeatedly that you should write about things of which you have personal knowledge, I drew on my own time in Canberra working for a Federal MP and my travels to Egypt for this story."

Visit my website at:
http://www.ritaleechapman.com

Printed in Great Britain
by Amazon